D1383802

CRISIS MOON

MICHAEL McGRUTHER

HOSEL & FERRULE BOOKS

Copyright 2020 © Michael McGruther

ISBN: 978-0-578-59870-3
Library of Congress Control Number: 2019916842

For Michele

*There is no strife, no prejudice, no national
conflict in outer space as yet. Its hazards
are hostile to us all. Its conquest deserves the
best of all mankind, and its opportunity for
peaceful cooperation may never come again.*

—JFK, Rice University, 1962

The Future

SATELLITE REPAIRMAN

JIM FELT THE first hot sting in the bottom of his foot, but the spacesuit wasn't reporting any issues.

"Capcom… my whole left side… intense pain, I don't know what…"

A barrage of stings began striking his body, making it difficult to talk.

"Something's hitting me, Capcom, needles—everywhere," he said through clenched teeth.

Being tethered to a satellite 22,223 miles above Earth allowed him the freedom to float when he needed a break, so he remained still, facing Earth, as waves of mystery pain swept over him.

The helmet static crackled, and a voice replied.

"All systems are normal down here, Jim. Are you messing with us again?"

"Not messing," grunted Jim as he rolled over and faced an undulating cloud of space junk, slowly spiraling toward him like a swarm of metal death birds circling their prey.

"Must abort! In a space junk storm! Must abort!" yelled Jim.

Heart pounding, he released the satellite tether as

thousands of tiny holes burst all over the spacesuit. His air supply leaked out in multiple directions.

Jim remained tethered to his spaceship, still intact a few hundred yards away. He started pulling toward the hatch and saw the lights from major cities across Europe blacking out.

Nothing but static in the helmet now.

"Capcom, what's happening down there? Does anybody read me?" said Jim.

Dead air.

A dagger-size shard of metal shaved past his visor, making him keenly aware that his head could be pierced like a cocktail olive at any moment. He reached out and grabbed the airlock hatch. Shrapnel bits shot by with greater frequency. With his left hand, he clamped on to his ship; with his right, he grabbed the airlock crank, spinning it and praying at the same time.

"Hail Mary, full of grace. The Lord is with thee."

From the corner of his eye, he saw the satellite he had been working on get obliterated, sending a chunk zooming his way like a cannonball. He let go of the ship and kicked off while grasping the tether. The satellite missed him by inches. He pulled hand over hand back to the ship, diving headfirst into the open hatch.

A tumbling shard of satellite clipped his left shoulder, tearing his spacesuit open and leaving a deep gash along his back. He clenched his jaw in agony as the pain of freezing temperatures hit his skin while his blood boiled into the vacuum of space.

Jim's breathing became labored; he was almost out of spacesuit oxygen. A thick cloud of shrapnel swarmed around him, but he managed to pull the hatch and close the airlock before taking on more damage.

Globs of blood from his wounds floated inside the small spaceship, bursting as they hit the walls, making the cabin resemble a murder scene. He strapped himself in and jabbed at buttons on the control panel to initiate the spacecraft's return engines. Jim tried to contact Capcom one last time.

"Capcom… if you can read me, I'm coming in hot and heavy, initiating auto return with full emergency systems operational. I do not know… if I'm gonna make it home… please tell my mom I love her," he said.

The small spaceship took heavy damage as the return engines fired up red-hot. Jim pushed the throttle forward while passing out on the control panel, racing back toward a darkened Earth on a preprogrammed flight path, emergency beacons flashing.

THE ADMINISTRATOR

A FLASH IN the sky blinded Richard Freed as he drove down the swamp-lined road to the gate of Kennedy Space Center's government-employee entrance. The bright intensity forced him to pull over and close his eyes. When he opened them and peeked through the windshield, it was a normal overcast Florida sky. No scheduled launches from SpaceX, Blue Origin, or NASA took place today, so he was baffled by the sudden light show. He put his car in gear and continued toward the gate, tucked behind a thick wall of overgrown swamp trees.

The fabled space agency was always underfunded, and the closer Richard got to the government offices, the more it showed. NASA once led at both launching rockets and inspiring the nation, and now in the year 2024, the time had come to reclaim greatness under Richard Freed, NASA's second African American administrator. He had been hired to transform the agency by a newly elected president with a mandate and a bold vision for American enterprise in space—a vision that kept getting cast aside during the previous decades of political turmoil, identity politics, and an expanding global welfare state.

Richard pulled up to the gate and noticed two guards in the booth, both looking at a computer screen, taking turns typing on the keyboard. Somewhat annoyed, he gave the horn two quick beeps. One of the guards looked up and raised a hand to say wait.

He sat patiently for three long minutes before hitting the horn again—and again was waved down. He watched the guards pick up the telephone receiver, handing it back and forth to one another like clowns doing a comedy bit.

"You have got to be kidding me," Richard mumbled to himself as he unbuckled his seat belt and stepped out of the car. Richard was a tall man with a baby face, which made him both imposing and kind at the same time. As he started walking toward the gate, one of the guards came out with a semiautomatic weapon at his side.

"Stay in your vehicle until we come to you. This is a restricted federal area, and we don't do tours back here anymore," said the guard.

Richard stopped walking and stood with his arms at his sides, flabbergasted. "What is your name, Soldier?" asked Richard, fumbling for the phone in his jacket pocket. The guard stiffened up and glared back at him.

"If you don't want to be arrested and removed from the premises, you need to sit in your vehicle while we deal with a technical difficulty. I will be with you shortly."

Another bright flash lit up the sky directly above them, unnatural and strange; then it faded out.

"You need to tell me exactly what is going on," said Richard as he tried to dial a number on his phone before realizing it was bricked, completely dead.

"Sir," said the guard.

Richard stepped close enough to read the guard's badge through the fence. "Officer Dowling. My name is Senator Richard Freed, and I have been put in charge of this bumbling agency by the president of the United States, so I'd advise you to open the damn gate and let your new boss in," said Richard.

The guard recognized the senator's face and lowered his weapon, embarrassed. "I am so sorry, Senator Freed. I didn't realize it was you, driving alone and all. We got a communications issue on our hands right as you pulled up."

A NASA jeep came speeding toward the post from within the fenced compound. The second guard came out of the post and stood on the deck watching the jeep. It skidded to a stop. A young man in a white button-up shirt and black glasses leaned out the window and said, "The space center is on lockdown, code red. No visitors whatsoever."

Dowling pointed his thumb at Richard standing on the other side of the gate. "What about your new boss, Senator Richard Freed?"

The young man got out of the jeep, walked over to the fence, and reached through to shake the senator's hand. "Senator Freed, it is an honor to finally meet you. I'm Allan Statter, and I head up the communications satellite division. We got a major problem happening in low earth orbit, sir." He focused on Dowling. "What are you waiting for? Open the gate for the new administrator!"

"We can't. Power's down," Dowling said with a shrug.

Richard stepped back toward his car while looking up at the tall fence. He opened the door, took off his jacket, tossed it in, and pulled out his cell phone charger. He pocketed it with his phone and rolled up his sleeves.

"Those flashes in the sky are not normal and may have something to do with communications being cut off," said Richard before taking a running jump onto the fence. He climbed fast.

As soon as Richard's rear hit the seat of the NASA jeep, Allan floored it, peeling out and leaving skid marks on the pavement.

"The satellites started to go off-line—boom, boom, boom—one after the other. We suddenly got cut off from Washington too. Everything is down. And I mean ev-ery-thing," said Allan as he navigated the pothole-ridden road past the old spaceship hangar toward a one-story white building with no markings.

"At approximately what time did you lose your first satellite link?" asked Richard.

"It happened a few minutes ago. Everything blinked off, poof. We don't even know what's the status on the ISS at this moment," said Allan, worried about the International Space Station.

Allan pulled a hard right at the end of the road and drove straight past the Vehicle Assembly Building with NASA's faded blue meatball logo painted on the side. Soon they pulled up to the Central Instrumentation Facility and ran inside the building. It was chaotic. Confused engineers yelled at one another in the satellite control room while technicians did their best to troubleshoot the situation in another room. No one had a clue about what was going on. Allan walked through the glass doors with Freed by his side and announced loudly: "Meet your new boss, everybody. Senator Richard Freed is here."

All eyes turned toward Freed.

"I understand we have a developing situation on our hands. We're going to have to make formal introductions another time. First, I need to know what you know," said Richard.

Navid, a young satellite technician, stood up and started talking. "It started when all of our military satellites went dark at the same time. The only way this could happen is if they suffered some kind of simultaneous hardware failure in orbit or more likely a direct attack of some kind."

"Like an electromagnetic pulse? I was blinded by bright flashes of light in the sky on my way in. When was your last contact with the ISS?" asked Richard.

"The ISS reported visuals of some LEO-zone explosion before being cut off," said another technician sitting at the ISS communications desk.

Richard leaned down and examined Navid's control station. The critical systems ran on backup generators, and all the computer screens flashed the same warning: *Connection to Satellite Lost*. Next to those words a timer counted how many minutes had passed since the event.

Outside the spaceship hangar, air force personnel descended on the space center from nearby Patrick Air Force Base. Soldiers with weapons started to take up positions as a precaution.

A young sergeant ran inside the Central Instrumentation Facility building shouting at the top of his lungs, "I'm looking for Senator Richard Freed!"

Freed walked out of the satellite control room, knocking back the young sergeant with the door.

"Senator Freed?" asked the sergeant, short of breath, a concerned look on his face.

"I'm Senator Freed. I hope you're here to tell me what in God's name is happening to our space assets."

"I'm here to transport you to Washington. America is under a space attack. The ISS is gone. The president is summoning you for an emergency meeting."

Freed turned to Dowling. "You're in charge until you hear from me. Nobody leaves, and nobody comes in."

"Yes, sir," replied Dowling as Freed and the young sergeant ran toward a waiting jeep. They both climbed into the back, and it sped off.

THE SELENOLOGIST

CHRISTINE UY LOVED the work but hated the office. The best the government could give the world's leading selenologist (lunar scientist) was a musty basement office deep in a forgotten wing of NASA headquarters in Washington, DC. She'd held this not-so-important position for the past three years, and her frustration was building. Christine's books had been on the *New York Times* bestseller list for her insights about the moon and its impact on global climate change—yet the most she'd been able to squeeze out of NASA was minimal funding for more speeches and PR stunts meant to grow interest in a return to the moon... in time. In how much time was the big unanswered question. Government time, as Christine had learned, can move very slowly indeed. While the public was teased with slick Hollywood-style videos that painted a picture of NASA possessing the technology to lead in space, Christine knew the reality was a decade away, and it depressed her more and more each day.

She got up from her desk, loaded a coffee pod into the machine in the corner of the small office, then waited, lost in her thoughts. Behind her, a picture of the moon was taking a long time to download on a wide computer screen. When not writing books, Christine spent her days mapping various changes in the lunar surface using weekly pictures from satellites orbiting the moon. She's monitored moonquakes and asteroid strikes and failed lunar landings by other nations. Today's picture took a long time to download and she was unaware of what was happening beyond her office walls.

"You sure do look sexy when you're thinking."

Christine pressed the button, creating the pop-and-hiss sound of an espresso machine. Her boyfriend, Jerome Jennings, MD, was standing in the doorway, dressed up and holding a small bouquet.

"Hey, how did you make it past security?" asked Christine. She walked over, took the flowers, sniffed them, and pecked him on the lips.

"This is the one-year anniversary of the day we met, and I wanted to surprise you. I arranged the clearance a week ago, and we have a reservation at Centrolina in one hour," said Jerome.

Christine put the bouquet in an empty vase on the shelf. "Aw. You're so sweet."

She dropped her eyes to mask that she had forgotten today was their anniversary. She was aware of time blazing by, and now he wants to be closer, which is great, but work demanded all her attention.

"I can't leave until this last section of the image downloads and I catalog it. There've been some strange anomalies lately," said Christine.

"It looks frozen," said Jerome.

"The satellite that snapped the picture sent it back, then went off-line. That has never happened before," she said.

"Leave it for tomorrow, babe. Bust out of here early for once."

"I can't."

"What you do isn't really critical around here. Maybe it's time to leave this dead-end gig and just write books full time? Come live with me in Miami. Try out us," he said.

Christine wasn't listening. She spotted something peculiar on her screen as her computer downloaded the final bits of the picture.

"Miami is going to have to wait, Jerome," she said, sitting back down in her chair and sliding close to the monitor. She used the keyboard to zoom in on a shadowy area.

"Babe, I can't wait forever," he said.

Christine sat up straight in her seat. "Oh my God," she said while looking closely at the monitor again. She isolated and enlarged the lower-left corner. "Oh. My. God… Jerome… do you see this?" She reached back to pull him by her side, but he was already gone.

She picked up her desk phone and pressed a button without taking her eyes off the image. "This is Christine Uy. I need to speak to Administrator Freed as soon as possible," she said before realizing nobody was on the other line. She hung up and tried again. Same dead connection.

She pressed the Ctrl and P keys to print the close-up area. Her office lights flickered. She grabbed the picture as it came out of the printer, slid it into a manila envelope, and ran out of her office. The hallway lights turned off as the building lost power. She swiped her iPhone flashlight on and ran to the stairway exit, opened the door and started climbing the stairs.

THE RESCUE

THE TEXAS SATELLITE Repair Company compound is well hidden in the foothills of the Los Coyotes region of Texas at the very edge of civilization, with open desert to the north and South Padre Island to the east. The team at Texsat planned for and rehearsed the emergency recovery of the Texsat Space Repair Module on a regular basis. In the event the module ever suffered a catastrophic system failure, or its pilot became incapacitated, there was a series of steps taken to ensure the retrieval of the spaceship and to save the life of the pilot. When the power went out across much of the United States, the Texsat Capcom team lost its satellite-based communications connection with the TSRM in orbit. Emergency procedures were initiated.

There was a sudden flurry of activity as the on-call medical team arrived at one of the small, unassuming buildings on the Texsat compound that housed a medical bay. Part of the team went inside and prepped the micro-hospital with two beds and all the necessary equipment and supplies, while a three-person team of one doctor and two nurses climbed into a tall white van. Its windows were tinted and an orange pyramid was painted on the door with a yellow

"T" in the middle and the phrase *Texsat—Getting You There and Back Again* written in bold letters on the bottom. The words *Search & Rescue Unit* were painted in crimson letters on the side. The van drove itself a short distance down a central paved road toward the tall Mission Control building at the end.

Doors burst open when the van pulled up, and Jance McIntosh—an older and imposing man with broad shoulders, white hair, and an old-fashioned curly mustache—ran out, accompanied by Dale York, a short, balding, middle-aged man with a round protruding belly. They rushed down the stairs, white-faced and dead serious. Jance fails to light his half-smoked cigar, before tossing it into a garbage can.

"I really should quit anyway," said Jance.

Dale pointed to the iPad he was carrying, concerned about what he was seeing. "The module is coming down faster than it should. We gotta brace ourselves for the worst-case scenario."

Jance glanced up at the sky and shook his head. "The only way Jimmy could have initiated the return flight is from inside the cockpit, which means he's in there and was able to perform a final step."

They made their way to the van idling at the end of the sidewalk.

"The question is if he misses his target, how much of an impact can he survive?" said Jance.

"I don't even think Superman would live after hitting solid ground in the module. God help him," said Dale as he climbed in the driver's side door while Jance went around to the passenger side. Both doors closed automatically.

Built into the van's dashboard was a tracking system. It

linked up with Dale's iPad and showed the spaceship's flight map. The medical team waited silently in the back. One of the female EMTs stared at the empty stretcher, mentally preparing for the job.

"You are folks I never wanted to meet under these circumstances, but here we are," said Jance as he pushed a few buttons, swiveling the chair around to face everyone. The self-driving van oriented itself to the spacecraft's projected crash site and started to drive out to meet it. They had practiced a dry run of this very scenario many times before, but the somber and depressing mood during the ride was palpable.

In very little time they entered open desert, navigating the winding, rugged hills behind the compound. The van was designed to handle it all. Equipped with custom tires fitted with spikes and chains and the maneuverability of a tank, the van could reach the remotest locations with relative ease.

The monitor displayed live progress of the ship's reentry trajectory by using old-fashioned radio technology that didn't depend on satellites. The redundant tracking system worked because the TSRM performed repair work in low earth orbit and always maintained a low-frequency signal.

"He's picking up too much speed—the reentry shield is at risk of failure," said Dale, helpless as he watched the module track closer.

"Why is he accelerating? This is suicide," said Jance.

"He's approaching max pressure threshold," warned Dale.

Being inside the Texsat module was like being in the center of a star: blinding light from the cascading fires of reentry made everything glow orange-red. Jim's wounded and bloody body floated in a sea of flashing light, making him look like a baby in a womb of fire. His eyes were shut and he was breathing ever so slightly. Every few seconds he flinched a little—slight movements, signs of life.

From the outside, the TSRM appeared like a fat missile with a cockpit. There was a viewport, and the top of Jim's helmet with the Texsat logo was clearly visible. His head bobbed as the spaceship slammed into Earth's atmosphere, tumbling and spinning its way back down.

In the rescue truck, Dale monitored the dash screen with great concern. "The module is way off course and not heading for any planned trajectory. He's going to land somewhere in the Gulf of Mexico instead."

Jance pressed a button on the dash and was connected to mission control via radio chat. "Dispatch the water rescue team. New coordinates are being sent over," he said.

"Roger. Coordinates received. Air team is being dispatched."

Jance pressed another set of buttons and the screen split into four different views, full black except for a blinking red dot in the center of each.

On top of the van, a box resembling a luggage container slid open, and four small drones lifted off and zipped ahead at incredible speed. The drones flew over rocky terrain, up and over a hill, and through small holes in trees—smart drones navigating with precision accuracy by remote control operators back at mission control.

Jance, Dale, and the medical team watched the live video feed as drones went down an incline, leveled out, and flew toward the gulf.

"Brace yourselves for UFO sighting videos soon to be popping up on the internet," quipped Dale.

The beach was calm and quiet this afternoon. A young couple enjoyed their walk with mugs of coffee in hand, while their two dogs frolicked in the water beside them.

An eerie distant whistling sound started coming from the sky and was all part of the design. Jim had created the safest spaceship for constant commercial use, including recovery systems in the event of an emergency. The whistle was designed to help pinpoint the crashing spaceship's location by the flying drones, which now locked on to the sound and buzzed toward the beach.

Both dogs stopped frolicking and cocked their heads up toward the sky, but the couple had yet to hear anything. Soon, a bright light soaring like a meteor streaked over the horizon. The silver body of the ship reflected the sun and could be mistaken for an incoming ICBM. The dogs barked and ran in circles. The couple peeked up, sheltering their eyes through their hands; thought they were about to be bombed; and ran away from the water, splashing coffee before dropping the mugs altogether.

The TSRM torpedoed into the water behind them, skipping like a stone and shooting off into deeper waters as if it had been thrown by a giant. The nose of the module clipped the water, causing it to tumble head over heels, fast, until it slammed to a rest and floated about two miles from shore, steam rising along all sides.

The Texsat drone fleet zoomed above the water with their sensors locked on the ship. They hovered around it in a circular formation, each drone adjusting focus on the points of damage.

Inside the rescue van, a cheer erupted when the live video feed of the space module showed its intact passenger lying inside.

"His vitals are good—he's alive!" said Dale while letting out a long breath of nervous air. The other screens locked onto the ship's damage. Tiny computers mounted to the drones calculated the cost of repair and what supplies would be needed.

A Texsat rescue chopper arrived with a medical team aboard and hovered over the space module. One rescuer was lowered down on a platform with room enough for two people. The waves crashed, rocking the module. Onlookers gathered on the beach, taking video with their phones and gawking at the bizarre and unexpected event happening right before their eyes. Was it a NASA ship? An alien crash-landing? It was too far out for anyone to capture a clean image.

The rescuer balanced on the ship and pulled a thick black rod from his cargo pocket. The rod expanded into a multipronged crowbar. He pried the viewport window until it cracked open. He pulled away the broken glass and jumped down into the module. The ocean rocked the small ship, rolling it far to one side, then water rushed in and flipped it over so they were submerged.

Underwater, getting Jim out was now an urgent matter of life and death. The rescuer worked twice as fast while cold water filled up the cabin. He unbuckled and tugged at Jim but couldn't move him. The rescuer looked closer, determined Jim's left leg was stuck, swam down to investigate, and to his horror, found a giant shard of shrapnel pinning Jim's thigh to the wall of the spacecraft. The rescuer yanked and tugged, ripping Jim's leg muscles until he came loose. He picked up the shrapnel and slid the long metal shard under his side belt. There was Mandarin writing on it.

The rescuer swam around and up with Jim under his arm. When they surfaced, he pushed Jim onto the helicopter platform, then climbed on. Once secured, the platform reeled them up into the belly of the chopper as it flew away just as fast as it had arrived.

The Texsat module, now swallowed by the ocean, gave out a last gurgle of air as it sunk from view.

Aboard the chopper, the medical team cut what remained of the spacesuit off Jim, revealing a body peppered in thousands of painful-looking tiny red holes, some still smoking with hot metal that punctured but didn't penetrate deeper than the skin.

One of the young nurses gasped at the sight. "I know a third-degree burn when I see one," she said while getting antiseptic and gauze ready to apply.

"Probably why he went into shock," said the doctor, who rubbed his gloved fingers over some of the hot shrapnel.

"I want him heavily sedated long enough for us to clean every wound and operate on his leg," he said while the medical team hooked him up to an IV and oxygen. Jim's vitals remained stable. The goal was to keep him comfortable and pain-free until the helicopter landed back at the Texsat base.

The day turned out to be one of the hottest on record, with the setting sun hanging large in the sky. The helicopter doors opened, and the nurse wheeled Jim into the medical building. His operation lasted a little more than three hours and required two separate teams working in tandem. The various metals removed from Jim's body weighed more than six pounds in total and left him looking like a bloody golf ball covered in bandages. The shard pulled from his leg was cleaned, examined, and left on a side table in the recovery room. Outside, Jance waited for Jim's mother to arrive.

Angelique Lowe was a familiar face on the compound but never during a launch because of her built-in fear of one day witnessing something better left unseen. She knew Jance was like a father to Jim and watched him calmly puffing on a cigar as she pulled up in front of the building. Angelique made eye contact with Jance and started to cry as she got out of the car. "I drove here as fast as I could," she said.

Jance pulled her close and they hugged tightly. "Jimmy's going to be OK. He may not look so familiar in his bandages, but he's going to fully recover," he said while squeezing her warmly. She nodded and felt only a little relief.

"I need to be near him," said Angelique.

Jance took one last drag on the new cigar before stomping it out. "Yes, ma'am, but I'm warning you, he doesn't look as healthy as he actually is," he said.

Angelique took a deep breath and wiped her eyes. "I'm his mother. I can handle it."

Jance put his right hand in his front pocket and pulled out a small chunk of metal. He held it between two fingers and handed it to her. "His body was covered in these from the neck down, six pounds worth, all from destroyed satellites," he said.

She took the metal chunk and inspected it. "And not one of them made it into his head or heart? Praise the Lord."

"God keeps saving Jimmy for something else," said

Jance as he led Angelique into the medical bay through the front door.

Angelique gasped when she stepped into the room where Jim was asleep, as if she could feel the painful-looking bloody wounds covering her baby boy.

The doctor who had operated on him walked in from a side office and stood right beside her. "He's on enough medication to sleep through the worst of it. When he does wake up, he will not feel like himself for many weeks. He'll have to stay in bed. This is going to be a long, slow recovery period."

Angelique nodded, moving to Jim's bedside, waving her hand over his arm, not wanting to touch any of the wounds. "Thank you for helping him," she said to the doctor.

The physician closed his binder and removed his glasses, tucking them into his front pocket. "You can call me at any hour the moment you need something. I have to head back to the hospital to check on some other patients." As he turned to leave the room, Jance stopped in the doorway and leaned against the jamb, watching while Angelique neatened up the side table and tucked Jim in under the warm covers. Always a doting mother, her presence made the whole tragic unfolding of events much more tolerable.

PANIC IN WASHINGTON

ROOFTOP SNIPERS PEERED down from government buildings while armed drones buzzed the streets of Washington, DC, in a constant state of surveillance. Security around the White House was the most intense it had ever been, turning the compound into a high-tech military fortress that had never been deployed before.

Antiaircraft missile launchers were on the lawns and in the streets, and a small marine barrack was set up right outside the Oval Office. One by one, military leaders and government officials arrived at the White House and were escorted into a secure bunker where the president was being inundated with intelligence reports.

Richard marveled at the layers of military security as his car was searched at the gate. Whatever happened must have been an act of war, he thought. He heard someone shouting behind his car and peeked back at Dr. Christine Uy arguing with two MPs who wanted to hear none of what she had to say. She waved a brown manila envelope with one hand. Richard was familiar with Dr. Uy's work and knew if she made it all the way to the White House in the middle of this chaos, she had something important to share. He rolled down the window of his limo and asked, "Dr. Uy, what are you doing here?"

Christine turned around and recognized him in the limo as it was being searched. "Senator Freed, thank God! I tried calling you earlier," she said as she pushed past the guard and walked toward his window. "You have to bring me with you. I spotted a lunar anomaly and you need to look for yourself. You're not going to believe it."

"She's with me," said Richard to the MP while opening the door and waving her in.

"Thank you," said Christine.

"I'm willing to believe anything that explains what happened today. An anomaly on the moon? Get in. You're coming with me," he said.

The taller MP stopped her with his hand to her chest, pushing back. "I don't care who you are with, you are not authorized to enter the White House at this moment."

"Take your hands off me! I am trying to do my job," she said.

"Let her go. She works for me and needs to be in the briefing," yelled Richard from the back seat.

The MP waited for his partner, who nodded approval.

"Hands at your side," said the MP.

Christine looked at Freed and silently mouthed "thank you" while the guard patted her down.

"You can go," said the MP.

"Have a nice day," said Christine as she climbed in the back seat with Richard and closed the door. The limo pulled through the gate and headed into underground parking near the side entrance. Christine handed the envelope to

Freed without saying a word. He opened it, slid out the printed picture, and eyed it. "Is this for real?" he said.

Inside the White House bunker, the brightest minds tried to piece together theories about who, why, and how the nation's entire satellite network was taken down when the red telephone rang. Everyone stopped talking and focused on the lone working phone line. It was the emergency line used only by world leaders in a time of global crisis.

President Graves, a broad shouldered and hawk-eyed man, cleared his throat and picked up the receiver. "This is the president of the United States."

A distant-sounding staticky line crackled and hissed. A voice with a thick Mandarin accent sounded as if it came from within a tin can.

"Mr. President, my name is Commander Liu Zhou, and I am calling with the help of our only working satellite on behalf of Premier Xian. Please accept our deepest apology. The Chinese military had a major accident with our space program. One of our satellites exploded and caused a sub-orbital chain reaction. This mistake is what wiped out global communications. We are going to fix it and make it right."

The president pressed hold while looking across the table at Secretary of Defense Reardon, a career military man with expert knowledge of the Chinese military and space program.

"Could one satellite set off a chain reaction this significant?" asked the president.

"It is possible but highly unlikely. This points to a deliberate and hostile act on our space assets," said Reardon.

The president pushed the hold button again and asked, "Did you say one of your satellites exploded in orbit?"

"Yes. We had one very bad problem with an advanced weather satellite. Fixing it soon so global communications can be brought back online. World will have to rely on Chinese telecom sats for now. Premiere Xian will be calling you next after notifying all world governments of our mishap. Do not worry. Chinese military has total control of the situation," replied the tinny voice. The line went silent.

Richard and Christine entered the room and all eyes turned to them.

"Richard Freed. You're the man I've been waiting for," said the president.

"I'm not the person you need to hear from; Dr. Christine Uy has something to show you," said Richard.

"Who are you, Doctor?" asked President Graves.

"I'm a selenologist at NASA headquarters—it's a fancy word for a moon scientist, Mr. President."

"What does the moon have to do with our satellites being destroyed in orbit?"

Christine looked at Freed, who nodded. She set the envelope down on the table and pushed it toward the president.

He picked it up, slid out the picture, and saw the set of boot prints on the moon. "What's this? What am I looking at?"

"Those are fresh boot prints located in a place where no human being has ever set foot before, yet there they are, clear as day, on the southernmost part of the moon, marching off to who knows where," said Christine.

President Graves passed the picture around the room. Every military and intelligence official studied it in amazement.

"This situation just went from bad to nightmare, Mr. President. Only three nations are capable of landing people on the moon: Us, Russia, and China," said one of the joint chiefs as he passed the picture.

"How do you know these are new?" said Secretary of Defense Reardon.

"My work has been focused on solving the mystery of transient luminous phenomena near the lunar south pole for over a year and I've studied pictures weekly from a classified recon satellite. Last week the boot prints weren't there. The recon satellite is now off-line too—this was the last image it sent back," said Christine.

"How far out does the lunar recon satellite orbit around the moon?" asked Reardon.

"One thousand miles from the surface," said Christine.

The secretary leaned back, thinking for a quick moment. "The moon is more than two hundred thousand miles from Earth. There is no reason for that satellite to be off-line too. The Chinese are lying, Mr. President. This is intentional. They're up to something on the lunar surface and don't want anyone to find out; they've blinded our eyes in the sky."

"Any guess what they could be doing up there?" asked the president.

"Probably the same thing they do down here—land grab to expand their military influence and the communist agenda," said Reardon.

The president stood up and walked around the room, looking increasingly angry. "How did another country land people on the moon without US intelligence knowing a lick about it? This is an unacceptable, fatal failure in homeland security. An embarrassment for the first nation that put a human on the moon!"

President Graves leaned on the table and sternly took in all the faces of his team, ending with Richard and Christine who stood still at the opposite end.

"I want an equally brazen response," said the president. "We need to retaliate by landing Americans on the lunar surface ASAP. How certain are we that the Chinese are acting alone?"

Richard jumped in. "Those are Chinese taikonaut boot prints. When I was an astronaut in training years back, we spent time alongside rookie taikonauts before their first Shenzhou flight. I recognize the pattern of the boot print. That same pattern covered the sand at the edge of the lake where we practiced low gravity maneuverability."

"You didn't train in a swimming pool?" asked the president.

"NASA was concerned about potential theft of advanced technology used in the indoor facility. Practice sessions were only allowed in the older, fresh water training ground," said Richard.

"If you're right, the real question now is why are they secretly putting humans up there, in that specific location?" said the president.

"The lunar surface is mineral rich. Rare moon minerals that can't be found on Earth are probably what they are after. I'd bet my life on it," added Christine.

One of the joint chiefs leaned back in his chair. He was an old-timer with wisdom and experience going back to the Cold War. "It really doesn't matter why. Fact is, it's illegal for any nation to occupy the lunar surface per the 1967

Outer Space Treaty. If you want to act, Mr. President, you have all the legal grounds needed to," he said.

"I have no choice in the matter. We must mount an emergency operation to the surface of the moon, or communists will secure a foothold and control it. I'm not letting that happen on my watch," said President Graves.

"I'll gather the best CIA minds on this," said Buck Smith, the director of the CIA.

"Something this big is going to take more than the CIA. We'll need all our resources and agencies working together, led by the Space Force," said Reardon.

The president shook his head while looking at Richard. "No. We're not going to flex our military might. Let's play this out smart. We are in a battle of economic systems, and that's why I'm putting you in charge, Richard. I need you to get a spaceship to the moon without anyone knowing about it. That's step one."

Richard nodded, feeling the pressure landing squarely on his shoulders. "Getting to the moon unnoticed... is step one?"

"America alone? How are you going to enforce the Outer Space Treaty without first going to the UN?" asked CIA Director Smith.

"We're not. China works in shadows and we will serve justice in shadows. Whatever they're working on up there has to be destroyed. I'll leave those methods up to you and Richard," said the president.

Richard swallowed hard and stood tall, straightening his suit. "Thank you, Mr. President. I'll have an outline of a plan of action on your desk by morning."

Richard and Christine hustled down the halls of the

White House together. She thought he made an insane promise and knew getting humans to the moon was still years away, tied up in massive government bureaucracy. The Space Force was not yet a fighting outfit either. No spaceships, no weapons, meant it was still mostly relegated to ground based support work.

"How are you going to pull this off when NASA doesn't even have an operational spaceship?" asked Christine.

"I'll find someone in the private sector. Someone with the capability and the balls to be recruited for the mission," said Richard.

"SpaceX? Blue Origin? They're not even close to being ready to send humans into orbit, let alone to the moon," said Christine.

"Others are out there. I'll find the right partner," Richard said.

"What can I do to help?" asked Christine.

"Start by putting together a list of all the tools and equipment needed to determine exactly what minerals and raw materials are near those boot prints," said Richard.

"You'll need more than gear. It takes a trained eye to perform the work I do," said Christine.

"When I find a company willing to transport people up, you're going," said Richard as they exited the White House together.

Christine stopped walking, frozen in shock. Her whole world turned upside down. Richard was getting in the limo when she snapped out of it. She ran to catch up. "Did you just say that I'm going to the moon?"

"Who else can do what you do? We need to know for certain what is so damned valuable up there," he said.

As the limo left 1600 Pennsylvania Avenue, Christine's smile reflected in the window; her gaze fixated on the moon as they sped through the empty streets of Washington, DC.

CHESS

THE AMERICAN PUBLIC was kept in the dark after the world experienced its first globally catastrophic event in space. At first, it was only an inconvenience of lost internet, cell service, or power. News media and those dialed into geopolitical affairs filled the void of the unknown, theorizing electromagnetic pulse weapons had at long last been used against the United States and World War III was now imminent.

The Press Secretary's daily conferences fueled speculation. Media were informed that military measures would be taken in every state as a matter of national security, out of an abundance of caution. On the surface, to the general public, nations seemed to be cooperating in the satellite rebuild effort. China was at the forefront, a hero for reestablishing communications for poorer nations first. Although there was no bona fide military threat, tensions remained at a critical level around the globe.

To soothe the public, government agents went across the nation holding town hall discussions with local communities on public safety in the new space age. United States postal employees began delivering instructional leaflets. The information was sparse and warned only of a continued high volume of space junk persisting, possibly for more months to come. Entire families moved into their basements. Predictably, looting increased as criminals took advantage each nightfall. Conspiracy theorists came out of the woodwork as the days progressed, and a general sense of doom and uncertainty swept the nation.

The news was filled with horror stories of people who either didn't heed the warnings or had extremely bad luck. The car-size chunk of satellite that slammed into a lone mountain climber in Colorado seemed the most random and unlucky of all.

"The Lord is coming. Repent your evil ways before the time is up!" warned a man standing outside of the White House with his briefcase at his side. Halfway down the block from him another prophesied an alien invasion, claiming himself humanity's savior, the sole owner of alien plans emailed to him in 2009.

This scene repeated in different countries, cities and rural towns alike. Countries deployed military forces wherever they held a foothold, standing ready. The farther the geopolitical standoff spread, the less people felt at ease. Diplomats and military officials communicated with one another via landlines, each assuring the other they had no intention of provoking a ground war unless attacked first.

The Chinese were very convincing about their peaceful motives and quelled some of the fears with their allies. US intelligence knew better and was having none of it.

The president approved the use of CIA black budget funds on the clandestine mission, code named Operation Red Moon. In his mind, the only way to ensure that it remained hidden, was to limit knowledge to a small number of trusted insiders. Richard submitted his resignation from his official role as NASA administrator to give it the semblance that private enterprise was behind the mission, not the US government. The president dispatched Colonel Lou Stetz, a trusted CIA insider, to canvass potential candidates for the mission, while Dr. Christine Uy was given a new office down the hall from Richard's, where she prepped for the scientific research trip of a lifetime. It was not lost to Christine that if she had left with Jerome before the picture finished downloading, she might not be on the cusp of realizing her childhood dream of being the first woman to walk on the moon.

WAKING UP

Jim's eyelids fluttered. His eyes watered, as he took in the dimly lit room. He recognized the familiar rolling hills of his ranch property through a crack in the drawn shades. He was home and in his own bed, medicine bottles stacked high on the side table. Tubes extended from his forearm, tethering him to an IV. *What the heck happened to me,* was the first clear thought that popped into his head.

Attempting to sit up caused instant pain, forcing him to lie right back down. Gritting his teeth and staring at the ceiling, Jim gathered strength, pushed through the agony, and tried again. Taking a couple of deep breaths, he steeled himself, then let out a tortuous howl while using both arms to hoist himself up until he was sitting upright.

"You're awake, Jimmy!" said Angelique from another room.

"Mom?" he said as Angelique ran into the room and stood in the doorway with both hands over her mouth.

"You're awake. Don't move," she said while walking to the windows and pulling open the shades to let the daylight in.

Following right behind her, tail wagging, was Apollo,

a small black Lab who leaped up and landed on the end of the bed. He started licking Jim's toes in affection. Angelique located a cord hanging on the side of his bed.

"Gentle, Apollo, gentle," said Angelique while pressing the control panel's up button with her thumb. The head of the bed rose up, so Jim was sitting without straining.

Apollo's toe licks made Jim giggle, he patted him on the head. "Hey, Apollo. How's my doggie." Jim looked over at his mom and reached for her hand. "What happened to me, Mom?"

"You don't remember? You had a pretty bad accident in orbit. You got hit by something up there and escaped. Everybody is so thankful you survived in one piece," she said.

"Me too. But how long have I been out of it?"

"Over two weeks now… in and out of it but never fully awake."

"What happened to the ship I was in?"

"It sank to the bottom of the Gulf of Mexico."

Jim pulled up his sleeves, inspecting the many healing scars that pitted his forearms for the first time. He looked under his shirt finding deeper red bumps across his torso. He thanked God because he was extremely lucky to be alive. "Holy shrapnel," said Jim.

"You must be starving. The doctor said when you came out of the medication, hunger would be severe."

"My gut is like a bottomless pit, but what I really want is a black cup of coffee to shake this fog out of my head," he said.

"The fogginess is a side effect of the medicine, sweetie. You have no brain injury at all. Like I said, it's a miracle."

"You know I need my coffee, Mom," Jim whined, smiling his little boy smile for her.

"Coffee and a hot breakfast coming right up," she said. She kissed him on the forehead and walked out of the room with the purposeful gait of a loving mother caring for her child.

Jim took further account of his injuries while he waited. He rubbed his fingertips lightly over the red wounds on his arms and saw that his legs were in worse condition. A shard of shiny metal on his side table glinted in the sunlight. He picked it up to examine it.

"That was pulled right out of your left leg," said Angelique as she returned and handed Jim coffee in an old NASA mug, which had been broken and glued back together. His favorite from a childhood stay at space camp.

"I got nailed with space shrapnel and lived to tell about it," said Jim.

"Wrong space at the wrong time is the way Jance described the accident to me. Do you have any recollection of what happened?" she said.

All Jim could muster was a foggy image of himself working in orbit. He took a couple of sips and smiled at the taste of his favorite drink. "Last thing I remember is repairing a satellite, same as I always do. Everything else is a blank." Jim pointed to the hundreds of tiny red dots all over his arms. "What did they do with all of the shrapnel that was in me?"

Angelique picked up a bottle of prescription lotion from the side table and rubbed his wounds, her hands soft with age. "Kept it at your office in a box. Over six pounds of metal fragments in all."

Jim pulled his sleeve back down, his gaze lifted as he reflected. He took another sip of coffee. "Now it's coming back to me… there must have been an explosion right in the LEO zone. I kinda remember seeing a bright flash. Not the space station I hope."

"The ISS and everyone on board didn't make it," she said somberly before handing him the remote control.

"Here. Put on the TV and you'll hear the whole story. Crisis in space is the only thing on the news now that the stations are back on the air. The whole thing's really tragic, Jim. I hope you'll think twice about going up again."

"This all happened in two weeks?" he asked.

"You catch up on the news, and I'll be right back with your food. I called Jance and told him you're awake. He's on his way over."

"Mom, you're the best," said Jim as she left the room. He pressed a button on the remote and a static-filled, jumpy broadcast of ABC News beamed onto the far wall from his projector. The words *Catastrophe in Space* scrolled across the bottom of the screen while a panel of scientists and government officials updated the public on their progress in getting global communications back up and running at full speed.

"Damn," Jim muttered to himself, dumbfounded, before sipping his coffee again. Apollo crept closer and laid along his thigh, watching the TV too. The roundtable discussion, complete with interactive maps and graphics, explained how an experimental Chinese weather satellite exploded in low earth orbit and set off an epic chain reaction of destruction.

"Weather satellite my ass!" yelled Jim.

It only took a matter of moments of watching the

broadcast for him to grasp the full scope of what had happened; the entire planet's satellite-dependent communications systems knocked out, causing weeks of global chaos while Jim was home sound asleep, recovering. The talking heads on TV argued, speculating alternative scenarios. The one thing they agreed on: this accident was inevitable as more and more nations and private citizens entered the space exploration race. Now the talks centered around how to avoid a similar catastrophe from happening again in the future, and the need for serious space legislation.

Low earth orbit had become way too crowded. With the ISS quadrupling in size to accommodate wealthy private citizens seeking thrilling adventure, the hundreds of spy satellites and emerging private aerospace firms launching experimental ships that cluttered Earth's orbit were bound to crash into one another. And when you crash one small automobile into another small automobile at 17,500 miles per second (the speed at which objects orbit Earth), then you are going to have catastrophic results with cascading effects. It made perfect sense to Jim, and the more he learned, the luckier he felt.

Vital military satellites were supposed to be armed with protective missiles, but nothing could stop a tidal wave of crushed and shredded metal. The accumulation of more than fifty years of humankind's space ambitions would, with the help of gravity, form into a deadly piece of orbital trash and one day become Earth's second moon.

Angelique came back carrying a plate overflowing with eggs, toast, and cut fruit. Seeing Jim and Apollo watching the TV together, she smiled. When Jim was in intensive care, she worried that the dog would be without his master. She had been wrong. "Here you are, dear. Eat up," she said.

The doorbell rang. Apollo leaped off the bed, hackles up, growling as he ran to the front door.

"That must be Jance. I'll let him in," she said.

FLY ME TO THE MOON

ANOTHER ALL-NIGHTER AT work had given Richard a stiff back. He stood up, stretched, walked over to the windows, and looked down at the early morning traffic pouring into DC. The iconic picture of the American flag on the moon hung behind his desk. He's been living in his office here at NASA headquarters for three weeks now; the clutter was evidence. This was supposed to be an office where senators and congressmen came to discuss space policy before heading off to expensive lunches around Capitol Hill. Instead, Richard's been locked away, scouring hundreds of archived spaceship proposals, many far-fetched, submitted to NASA from individuals or private aerospace companies over the years. From the start, it's been a rough, tedious search for a needle in the haystack find: a competent and relatively unknown aerospace firm operating out of the national spotlight and willing to get the job done.

Richard winced at the smell from a pile of take-out boxes overflowing the garbage can and cracked open one of the windows to let fresh air in. He rubbed his tired eyes, went back to the couch to take another look at the document he was reading when there was a knock on the door. "Come in," he said.

Christine walked in with her iPad in hand. "How's the search going?"

"I'm not finding anything remotely workable at this moment. It's driving me crazy."

"Did you happen to catch today's *Fort Worth Star-Telegram* cover story?" she said while handing the iPad to him. "Check out this crazy story about a guy who was in low earth orbit repairing satellites who got knocked down to Earth. He survived and is starting to remember what happened," she said.

Richard's eyes widened as he skimmed the article. "I know him, Jim Lowe," said Richard, still reading.

"Wait until you get to the part about his company and the picture of his spaceship," said Christine.

Richard kept reading, scrolling through details of the Texas Satellite Repair Company.

"You have to be kidding me. I can't believe it," said Richard.

"Can't believe what?" she said.

"Someone has to tell the *Star-Telegram* we need this story deleted from their web pages. He's perfect. He's the guy, and his company's perfect too, but there could be one major problem," said Richard.

"You're running out of options. What's the problem?" asked Christine.

"Jim Lowe doesn't like me. I mean he really doesn't like me. We enrolled in the astronaut program together in the nineties. Jim is an arrogant prick who blamed me for our shuttle mission not getting off the ground," said Richard.

"Oh," said Christine as she picked up the iPad and enlarged a chart from the article. "I thought you might find some potential in his spaceships" she added.

Richard grabbed the iPad and studied the fleet of rockets owned by Texsat Satellite Repair Co. At the top, sized to scale, was the space capsule that had taken Jim Lowe to and from space when he did his maintenance work.

"He operates a reusable ship and has more than one," said Christine.

"Look. The man is an aerospace engineering genius and one hell of a professional, but he also has no love for the federal government and considers himself a private-sector-only guy. He's so idealistic, he's rejected contracts that went to Musk and Bezos in the past," said Richard.

"He's a small-government, America-first type? Sounds perfect for the situation we find ourselves in," said Christine.

"He's borderline antigovernment. He called NASA a bureaucratic mess, responsible for limiting human potential in space," said Richard.

"I can tell you from my time here that he has a legit point. Appeal to the patriotic side of him," urged Christine.

Richard examined the spaceship graphic again, studying it, not allowing his personal feelings to disrupt the mission he was tasked with seeing through. Maybe there was a way to make this work. "You know what, you're right. I'm going to do that. I'll go pay him a visit and find out if he can be convinced," said Richard.

Because of the history he had with Jim, and because he knew full well Jim had loathed the federal government and especially those who abused its perks, a delicate approach was called for. No special aircraft, no military personnel,

only Richard in a rental car driving out to visit his old pal…
checking in on him after the accident.

Richard caught up on some sleep on the flight from
Reagan National to McAllen International Airport. The
drive into the countryside was beautiful, a needed respite
from the fluorescent-lit office back in DC. The light-blue
sky was streaked with wispy clouds stretching toward the
heavens. Juniper trees and wild sage dotted the sides of
rocky hills as he drove past, creating a textured landscape
full of color. Texas inspired him with its ever-expanding
horizons. No wonder the new private space sector favored
the southwest.

Richard drove for a long time down a county highway
before coming to a slight bend. Rounding it led him up and
over a steep hill and then straightened out into a valley on
the other side. He hadn't seen a home or ranch for miles as
he drove along the road until he came upon a metal sign on
the right-hand side. He pulled over and hopped out of the
car to look at the sign up close. It had a yellow "T" set inside
an orange pyramid with the words *Private Property—Keep
Out* in bold letters at the bottom. Behind the sign, a long,
steep gravel road disappeared over another hill. Richard
checked his GPS. This was the spot. He got back in the car,
turned up the gravel road, and drove on. He soon passed
another sign warning that trespassers risked being shot on
sight by an armed guard. He drove on anyway.

The rental car climbed up the steep hill, creating a dust
cloud, obscuring it from view. Richard peeked in the rear-
view mirror and saw the dust devil trailing behind him. He
slowed down some more, trying to lessen the impact of his
tires on the dry dirt road.

Once at the top, Richard stopped and let the cloud settle around his car. When it did, a small compound of buildings and roads down in a hidden desert valley appeared. The place was well organized, surrounded by a tall and imposing electrical fence. Two full-size launchpads jutted from the ground in the distant desert. It resembled a hidden military base.

"I'll be damned," muttered Richard as he put his foot on the gas again and drove down the gravel road toward the gate below. The deeper into the valley he drove the more colorful the rocky hills around him became. The red and brown hues popped in the sunlight.

He pulled up to the gate and was greeted by a muscle-bound, armed guard dressed in jeans, a black T-shirt, a black baseball cap, and sunglasses. The guard was out of his building to meet Richard before he even arrived. A pistol was strapped to the guard's chest, visible, ominously accessible. He approached the vehicle as Richard rolled down his window. "You must have made a wrong turn and you can't read, my friend. You're trespassing on private property. I advise you to turn around and head on back out the way you came," barked the guard.

"I have an appointment with Jim Lowe," said Richard. He kept both hands on the steering wheel and looked at the guard. "I'm an old friend, from NASA. He's expecting me."

The guard stepped back and opened the door to his booth, letting a German shepherd out. The dog purposefully ran three circles around the car, sniffing and searching every inch. Richard pressed the window button, making it go up enough to protect himself.

"Don't worry. He's not interested in you. I am. Step out of the car."

Richard looked at the guard before turning his head and facing the shepherd now sitting at attention right outside his door.

"I'm a government official," said Richard.

"And this is private property, buddy. Step out of the car and be searched if you want me to let you pass, or you've got five minutes to disappear before I make good on the warning signs you read on the way in," replied the guard.

Richard got out of the car and stood with his hands behind his head. The guard searched him, hands in pockets, patting down legs and arms, the whole routine. He took Richard's cell phone and put it in his own pocket.

"You can have this back when you leave. How do you know Mr. Lowe anyway?" asked the guard.

"From our NASA days. I made an appointment and he should be expecting me."

"He is," said the guard. Satisfied with the pat-down, he tipped his hat at Richard. "When I open the gate, drive through, turn right, and follow the road until you reach the last building on your left. Park anywhere. That's Mr. Lowe's office."

Richard reached out to shake the guard's hand, and the shepherd leaped from the ground to the hood of his car on the way to attacking Richard himself. The guard called him off with the wave of a hand.

Richard, shaken, got into his car. "Thanks," he said.

The guard chuckled as he opened the gate with the click of a button inside his booth. He called the shepherd back into the booth with him. "You have a good day now, sir," he said.

"You too," said Richard, annoyed as he put the car in gear and drove through. Once he passed the gate and started driving inside the compound, he finally grasped how sophisticated and well-funded Texas Satellite Repair Company really was. Jealousy crept in.

Each building he passed used glass to bring in the outside light. They were marked above each entrance with modern letters made of steel: HQ, The Satellite Shop, Propulsion, Commissary, Medical, and, lastly, Mission Control, which is where Jim's office was. The differences between Texsat, a profitable private aerospace company, and NASA, a government agency that always doubled as a political football held back by layers of red tape, were stark to Richard.

He parked in an empty spot behind Mission Control and sat for a moment, allowing the impressive facility with its two fully functional launchpads a few miles straight ahead, to sink in. Mission Control was an A-framed building jutting into the sky, the rear-facing area filled with offices, the launchpad-facing area enclosed by a five-story floor-to-ceiling window.

"Wow," he said with an exhale. He turned off the ignition, got out of the car, and walked up the short set of silver steel stairs to a pair of double doors, his image mirrored in reflective glass. They opened before he reached the top.

Jim stood in the doorway, arms crossed, looking down. "What in the hell brings an ass-kissing government suit like you all the way out here?"

Richard stopped, taken aback by the hostile tone of Jim's voice. The pair were night and day in contrast. Richard looked stiff in his suit, Jim, rugged in a T-shirt and jeans. "Very nice to see you too."

"This better be important," said Jim.

"It is. I read about what happened to you up in orbit and realized I had to speak to you in person about something I'm working on," said Richard.

"You're gonna have to make it quick because I don't have much time to give you today. Follow me," said Jim, who turned around and started walking into the lobby.

Richard followed him and saw blood spots showing through the back of his T-shirt.

"Do you know you're bleeding right through your shirt?" said Richard.

"Some of the wounds still break and bleed a little. I'm heading to sick bay to receive new bandages in about an hour."

Jim led him down the hall to a set of open elevator doors. They stepped inside a glass box held together by steel beams and lift wires. Richard spotted only two buttons "Mission Control" and "The Pinnacle." Jim pressed "The Pinnacle" and the doors slid closed. The elevator lifted and took them right through the middle of mission control, giving Richard a quick glimpse at an open room with rows of computer stations arranged in stadium-style seating and facing display screens on the aisles. This allowed for a wide-open view of the launchpad through the all-glass wall on the other side.

"Who's your primary financial backer?" asked Richard.

"Jance McIntosh, an investment banker and space enthusiast. He owns a forty percent stake in the business and works here too," said Jim.

"Your company is incredible," said Richard as the elevator lifted them to the pinnacle, which was really Jim's office. The doors slid open and Jim motioned for Richard to step out first.

Richard's eyes widened, impressed but insanely jealous at this point. Compared to his NASA hovel of an office, Jim's was spacious, modern, taking up the entire top floor, with huge windows looking out toward the desert and launchpads. Jim is the king of his own working space program. Designer, dreamer, builder—a Frank Lloyd Wright of aerospace.

"Grab a seat. You want a coffee?" asked Jim.

"Coffee is exactly what I need. I'm pretty exhausted from this confidential project I've been put in charge of by the President," said Richard as he walked toward two old converted cockpit seats that doubled as chairs in the middle of the room. Both were positioned across from a leather couch and could spin around 360 degrees. He sat in one and used his legs to swivel, taking in the details.

"Confidential?" said Jim.

One corner of the office had a wooden workbench covered with drafting materials and model-spaceship parts. On the shelf above, a highly detailed mock-up of Jim's reusable spaceship was displayed under a plexiglass cube. The walls not made of glass had pictures of Jim in space working on satellites—promo materials selling him as the world's best space handyman. This room is where multimillion-dollar satellite maintenance contracts were signed with corporations smart enough to realize the value of his services. Like any other machinery, fixing spacecraft is far less expensive than buying (and flying) new ones.

"I'm kind of speechless, Jim. What you've achieved here is remarkable," said Richard.

"Business is booming too. I expect it to triple since the space incident and all," said Jim from the coffee station. He picked up two freshly made pour-over coffees and joined Richard, who was busy playing with the dead buttons and control switches on the inside of his chair. He pressed a button and leaned back as if he were about to take off when Jim handed him a coffee in a Texsat mug.

"Thanks," said Richard as he straightened up and got serious.

Jim sat down on a leather couch across from him, put his boots up on the coffee table, leaned back, and waited. "So... what's this confidential project, what do you want from me?" asked Jim, eyeing Richard with great suspicion again.

Richard sipped the coffee then set the mug down. "I know you distrust the government and that you're a strong individualist," said Richard.

"Extreme individualist is the official title," replied Jim as he leaned forward and rolled up his sleeves, revealing the new texture of his skin.

Richard recoiled a bit. "How much of your body is scarred?"

"Seventy percent," said Jim. "The satellite incident is the one and only time I've been injured in space and it nearly killed me." He grabbed a tube of cream, squirted a dab into his palm, and rubbed it on his scars. "It itches like hell," said Jim. "As you were saying?"

"Yes. What brings me here. You know I was the acting NASA administrator until three weeks ago?"

Jim chuckled a little, then it turned into laughter from deep in his gut.

"What's so funny?" pleaded Richard.

Jim started laughing harder at Richard sitting in the oversize pilot chair, looking like a big kid who was way out of his league. Through chuckles, Jim said, "They made you the head of NASA, and you've never even been into space. That's the problem with the entire federal government right there. People who know nothing are in charge of those who do everything, and folks wonder why nothing gets done right."

Richard swiveled around, hiding his expression. He took offense to the comment because Jim hit a nerve. Jim left NASA after being in the astronaut program, and it paid off. Richard kept along the path of political power, which never pans out as expected. But here they are together again. Richard swirled back around. "We need your help, Jim," he said.

"What kind of help?"

"The accident you were in was no accident."

"It sure felt like one to me, and I was up there, you weren't. I remember seeing the explosion before the shrapnel storm."

"That's how it was supposed to look, like a major accidental space catastrophe unlike the world has ever seen before."

"How do you know?"

"While you were knocked out and healing, I was uncovering all the facts. We got a game changer unfolding. You're not going to believe what we discovered."

Richard pulled a folded piece of paper from inside his jacket and handed it to him. "What am I looking at?"

"Fresh Chinese taikonaut boot prints in the Aitken basin, deep in the south pole of the moon," said Richard.

"Nobody's ever been down there," Jim scoffed.

"The Chinese military knocked out global communications in order to cover up something they're working on in the basin."

"A moon base?" asked Jim.

"Intelligence thinks maybe a combo military and science outpost, but nobody knows how much land is being occupied."

There was a long silence while Jim let this sink in. He glanced across the room at a large framed picture of the US flag on the surface of the moon that he'd had since childhood. Such an iconic image was the reason he wanted to be an astronaut in the first place. "You need me to build a spaceship that can make it to the moon, don't you?"

"We have an urgent need to transport five people to the surface and return them home, undetected," replied Richard.

"Don't you already have contracts with SpaceX for missions like this?" asked Jim.

"They're busy rebuilding communications infrastructure and are already compromised by Chinese and Russian intelligence agents. I need someone under the radar, an extreme individualist, like you," said Richard.

"Five Americans on the moon. What's the mission going to entail exactly when they land," asked Jim.

"Recon, scientific data gathering, and the possible enforcement of the 1967 Outer Space Treaty with explosives," said Richard.

"Hot damn," said Jim.

"The Outer Space Treaty's most important function was

to both prohibit the placement of weapons in space and to limit the use of the moon and all other celestial bodies to peaceful purposes. If we find any structure of any kind up there, they're coming down by orders of the president of the United States," said Richard.

"This sounds crazy," said Jim.

"We live in crazy times," said Richard.

Jim's eyes lit up. His childhood space fantasy and his real-world capability were merging in real time, and his mind raced.

"You're looking to transport five people and explosives to the moon to enforce a treaty that prohibits the bringing of explosives to the moon?" said Jim.

"Correct," said Richard.

"And you wonder why nobody trusts the government," said Jim, holding his head low, contemplating.

Richard couldn't read him and was unsure if he was winning him over.

"Imagine the ramifications if we lost free access to the moon?" said Richard.

Jim lifted his head and nodded. "I know how important it is, and I can make this happen for you, but it won't be cheap," he said.

"Money is no issue here. The moon is the absolute highest ground, and the president will not let it fall under communist control," said Richard.

"Nor should we," said Jim as he rose from the couch and walked over to the window that looked out at the launchpads. "But I didn't build this aerospace company from the ground up, so it could be used one day to save NASA's ass."

Richard stood, walked over to the window next to Jim. "America's ass is what needs saving, Jim, and you're our only hope."

"There's only one way it's happening with me," said Jim, abruptly leaving Richard's side to cross around to the encased model of his space module. He stood still for a moment, focused on it. "I can modify one of my ships pretty quickly, and it'll be able to make it to the moon and back, but I have one nonnegotiable string attached," stated Jim.

"Name it," said Richard.

"I'm going on the mission, and I'm in charge. Nobody pilots my ship but me," said Jim.

There was a long silence as Richard considered the demand. This is not what he wanted to hear. "I can't promise that. The Department of Defense and the Department of Energy are both up my ass. You know how the chain of command works."

"Go find yourself another ride to the moon because I'm not answering to a bunch of government nitwits who are qualified only by how much ass they kissed on the way up," said Jim.

"Jim."

"What?"

"I'm sure I can work it out on my end. I wouldn't have it any other way as long as it means getting us to the moon. I just didn't think you'd want to take that kind of risk so soon," said Richard.

"Taking risks is what I do for a living. I may be a pacifist at heart, but I'll be dammed if we let the moon fall into the wrong hands. It's our only doorway to deep space."

"I couldn't agree more, that's why we have to act fast," said Richard.

"I'm going to need the specs on the individuals and the cargo, including explosives, weight, dimensions, precautions. Everything," Jim said.

"What kind of time frame can you work in?" asked Richard.

"Oh, I already have the spaceship we're going to use more than half-done. I started work on a new multi-man capsule a few years ago, and I could have it ready to fly in less than three months," said Jim.

"Jim… that timeline exceeds all expectations, you sure you can do it?" asked Richard.

"In the private sector I work at the speed of passion, not paperwork," said Jim.

"And you're lucky to live in a country that protects and defends your right to do so," said Richard.

"Amen to that. So how many crew, in total?" asked Jim.

"One scientist, two military, yourself, and one NASA astronaut," said Richard.

"Who's that?"

"That's me. I'm going up too," said Richard.

Jim eyed Richard up and down, eyes smiling as he sized up Richard's desk-friendly physique. "There's going to be training and preparation for everyone taking the ride."

"Understood. We can work out of—"

"We will do it all right here at Texsat," said Jim.

"Even better," said Richard.

"Under my direction."

Richard nodded again in agreement. He wasn't worried about Jim doing things halfway and had confidence that he would be committed to safety above all else. Convincing the military was his next battle. Richard held out his hand. "Does that mean we have a deal?"

Jim reached out and the two ex-rivals shook hands. "Damn right we do."

About twenty miles into the drive back to the hotel Richard's cell service returned. He made a phone call. It rang one time.

"Stetz here," said the voice on the other end.

"Hello, Colonel. Did you have a chance to look over my request?" said Richard.

"I have, and I know a couple of highly qualified folks that are perfect for this," said Stetz.

"I made a deal with a transportation company today, so you got three weeks to convince them," said Richard.

"It won't take me that long," said Stetz. "I'll catch the first flight out in the morning and will be in touch with you by 18:00."

NEW HORIZONS

TEXSAT EMPLOYEES WERE summoned to the Mission Control building for an emergency Sunday morning meeting with Jim. He never called a company-wide weekend meeting like this unless something significant was happening. Concern among the staff grew as hushed voices wondered if their best days were behind them and layoffs would begin. Jance McIntosh and Dale York were the closest to Jim, but even they were in the dark.

All essential spaceflight operations team members (105 people to be exact) were chatting in the stadium seats behind the rows of computer stations. Sunlight flooded in through the windows and created a long, slightly tilted shadow of the empty launchpad and gantry in the distance. It was an ominous image for everyone who worked tirelessly to help build this company. In light of the satellite incident, low earth orbit space vehicles like the ones they used were under intense scrutiny by world leaders at the UN General Assembly. Employees feared that the private space industry would be shut down just as it started to take off.

Jim walked in from a side door. His staff stood and applauded his obvious return to health. He was loved by the team he had assembled. For many, this was the first time seeing him walk on his own since the accident. He had a barely noticeable limp as he walked confidently toward them.

"Looking great, Jimmy!" said a voice from the seats.

"Welcome back, boss," said another voice.

Jim stopped at the center of the separation railing, so he could address everyone.

Jance mouthed to him, "Is everything OK?"

Jim nodded yes. He waited as the well wishes died down and folks stopped talking.

"Good morning, team Texsat," said Jim.

The collective "Good morning, Jimmy" in return was a tradition they had been using for as long as he'd addressed the company. He was their quirky leader, and his personality was evident throughout the campus. Working at Texsat was equal parts serious and fun.

Jim cleared his throat. "Thank you all for coming out here on your weekend. I called you in today because I have an important announcement to make that will impact every single one of you." As Jim surveyed the room, he caught nervous glances among the engineers.

"While I was laid up and still healing, I got a call from an old friend of mine wanting to reconnect. He recently served as the acting administrator of NASA and came all the way to my office to ask me if we at Texsat were capable of taking on a challenging government job—one that goes above and beyond the work we normally do repairing satellites. It turns out that NASA needs to send some scientists to the moon and back as fast as humanly possible. We're being asked to handle it because, quite frankly, we're the only ones who are capable. I called you all in here to inform you that I accepted the job, and because of that, everyone in this room is getting a fat raise starting now."

An audible sigh of relief got the whole room laughing. While this went on, Dale York leaned forward and said to Jim, "The moon, Jimmy? Are you freakin' nuts?"

"Every great project starts with you doubting me, Dale," said Jim. He focused on his employees again.

"All right, everybody, listen up. The job is subject to extreme national security measures and that means top secret clearance. Expect new rules we'll all have to follow for the duration of the project. This compound is already remote, but additional layers of security will be set up and hidden for several miles around our perimeter. I need all of you to take your oath of secrecy very seriously. We're a tight-knit group, and I know I can trust every single one of you, but any intelligence slipup could result in devastating consequences for us all."

Jance raised his burly arm and interrupted Jim. "When did you sell your soul to Uncle Sam without notifying any of us first? Have you gone and lost your mind in orbit?" he said.

After a few chuckles Jim leaned on the railing, crossed his arms, and continued. "Hey, I'm getting to the good part. The reason NASA wants to go to the moon so quickly is because they've got strong evidence that other countries have been secretly landing men up there for a while now, and nobody knows why."

The room fell silent.

"You're serious?" said Dale.

"Yes. I looked at the intelligence pictures with my own eyes. This is a real crisis."

"What have you gotten us into, Jimmy?" said Jance.

"We need to get our own people on the ground to investigate and come home with some evidence. That's where Texsat comes in," said Jim.

"How are we going to make this happen? You crashed the only working module we have," said Dale.

Jim waved both of his arms, and the giant TV screens on either side of him lit up with an image of the Texsat logo. He faced the screen, waved his right hand, and the image on the right changed to a schematic for a spacecraft called the Texsat Space Lunar Module, or TSLM. It was a highly detailed image of a sleek module that resembled an Apollo-era ship. "We're going to stop work on all projects and focus on speeding up completion on the Texsat Multinaut, which I'm now calling the TSLM."

Engineers were already taking notes.

Jance put on his glasses and eyed the picture with a healthy level of suspicion. "It can carry five astronauts plus supplies to the lunar surface. We're going to use our newest engine technology for space propulsion to shorten the travel time," said Jim.

"How much time to we have to complete it? The Texsat Multinaut is little more than half-done," said an engineer from the middle of the room.

"This spacecraft needs to be en route to the moon in twelve weeks. I want everyone to come to the office at your normal time on Monday and begin work like you normally would. The computers will be updated with a new timeline and tasks for every department. Any questions?" said Jim.

"What happens if we miss the target and can't launch a ship in time?" said Jance.

"We're not going to. Everything is already in place. It's a matter of a few tweaks, and then we follow our normal production process. I stayed up all night running the data before calling you guys in. It works out," said Jim.

"Are you sure you want to go back up into space so soon after what happened to you?" said Dale.

"I have to do this. We have to do this. What's at stake is beyond value—it's the gateway to the stars and an express ticket to making Texsat a global leader in the private space sector," said Jim.

THE RECRUITS

COLONEL LOU STETZ has done this job many times before. He owned unique friendships with a guarded list of highly trained individuals that the US government employed for specialist covert ops. These Americans had abilities that were right for Operation Red Moon. Stetz knew exactly who needed to be involved.

His day had started before sunrise in Washington, DC, but by midafternoon he had arrived at a small hilltop ranch home on the outskirts of Flagstaff, Arizona. When he drove up to the eccentric home and pulled into the gravel driveway, wind chimes danced on a nearby tree, while water from a crystal fountain trickled down into a koi pond off to the side. The property, surrounded by tall conifers juxtaposed against a blue sky, felt like a tranquil spot where an off-the-grid man-bun guy might commune with nature and grow his own food.

Stetz knew better, because the man who lived here was a deadly assassin with a record of killing several of the world's most wanted. The front door to the home was open. He walked onto the porch and knocked on the screen. He could look right through it to a back door that was also open.

"I'm meditating around back!" said a grizzled voice

from behind the house. Stetz chuckled and walked around the side, stepping carefully on a neatly arranged stone path that led to the backyard, where he found Hector Benevides sitting in a yoga pose on a mat in the center patch of green grass. Lit incense sticks stuck out of the ground and gave off a limey scent. At twenty-nine years old, Hector was tall, with a full beard and wild locks of unruly hair. His chest was bare but for a crucifix around his neck. He opened one eye to check out his visitor.

"Aw, hell no, dawg. Not interested," said Hector.

"What? I came to say hello," said Stetz.

"You never just stop by to say hello."

"I've been trying to call you, but you never answer."

"I'm a private citizen now. I don't answer calls from unlisted numbers," said Hector while Colonel Stetz walked closer until he was standing directly in front of him.

Stetz squatted to be at Hector's eye level and said, "What are you doing with yourself these days, Hec?"

"I already told you. I'm retired now, focusing on my inner peace and chakras."

"How's that working out for you?" said Stetz.

"Staying relaxed does not come naturally to me, but I'm getting there. I'm learning," he said.

"I think you better hear me out on what I have going on," said Stetz.

"You said that last time, and I ended up stranded on Mount Damavand for three weeks, drinking my own urine, barely clinging on to life. Like I said… not interested."

Stetz sat down cross-legged in front of Hector.

"Have you ever tried yoga, Colonel? It balances the whole body and mind."

"I'm old-fashioned. I drink whiskey."

"Yoga helps keep the chaos factory in my brain from taking charge," said Hector.

"I gotta admit, this is a pretty spot you have out here. I felt more mellow the second I heard those chimes," said Stetz.

"Right? I love those chimes much better than the sound of artillery. I don't ever want to leave my quiet place. I've earned the right," said Hector.

"Never?" asked Stetz.

"Never ever," said Hector.

Stetz anticipated this was going to be a hard sell so he was going to have to be creative with his pitch. He took in the daytime moon, clear and bright in the sky. He lingered on it for a moment, gathering his thoughts.

"Tell me something, Hec. Would you leave this planet if you could?"

Hector eyed Colonel Stetz with a half-crooked smile. "Have we been contacted by aliens? Because if they're aliens, that changes everything on my end," said Hector.

"Aliens? Not that I know of."

"Then why are you here?"

"The president needs you to go to the moon."

Hector lowered his arms until they were resting on his knees. He sighed. A concerned look settled in his eyes. "What's going on up there?" he said.

"Another country has been visiting a potential mineral-rich region on the lunar south pole called the Aitken basin and not telling anyone about it."

Hector was intrigued now. The idea of going to the moon was enticing to a man who initially signed up for service because he first came to know the military through video games, many of which were set in space. The fact that he turned into a highly decorated soldier had more to do with the time he was born than a natural evolution of his true self. Being deployed to the moon would be unlike any mission he'd ever been on, the icing on the cake of a brilliant military career. He was already half-sold.

"Will there be combat up there?" asked Hector.

"Nobody is anticipating it, but you'll be armed and ready just in case," said Stetz.

"What exactly are we going to do… if I go?"

"You're looking for buildings. Any man-made structures that are found, no matter the size, must be completely destroyed because it is a violation of international law for nations to build on the moon," Stetz said.

"You want to send me to enforce the law… on the moon," said Hector.

"You and four others."

Hector leaned back, thinking, looking out into the forest beside his home. "Who's been up there while we've been napping?" he said.

"China, Russia—or, worst-case scenario, both working together," said Stetz.

"Can't NASA do a flyby and take pictures of what they're up to?" asked Hector.

"Every satellite sent to look at the south pole on the dark side of the moon in the past five years has crashed or disappeared," said Stetz.

Hector stared at him, his expression changing as he understood the scenario. "What's the plan for getting to moon?"

"You'll go up in a small private-sector spacecraft. Undetected. Untraceable."

"This would qualify as the most hazardous job I've ever taken, Colonel. My rates are going to have to go up if you want me to come out of retirement," said Hector.

"How does five million paid in two parts work for you? Half when you start and half when you come home," said Stetz.

"That's a lot of loot. How long do I have to decide?"

"I need to know if you're in before I leave here. We are on an accelerated schedule. The whole job should take you around five weeks. Four spent training with the aerospace company and a three-day trip to the moon and back."

"A million per week," said Hector as he stood up, stretching his muscular arms into the sky, and for the first time noticing the moon hanging there. He stayed in that pose for a moment before looking down at Colonel Stetz.

"Hell, yeah, I'm a hundred percent in. Kicking commies off the moon sounds like a lot of fun if you ask me," said Hector.

Colonel Stetz smiled and stood up.

"I knew I could count on you. I'll be in touch soon. Take care of your private affairs and be ready to be transported to the training location in one week's time."

"Yes, sir," said Hector with a salute as Colonel Stetz turned and walked off.

"Hey! Don't you at least want to stay for a beer?" yelled Hector.

"Can't. I have to make it to my next sales meeting," said Stetz, already around the corner and out of sight.

As Stetz's car drove away Hector reached down to pinch

the incense out with his fingers. He rolled up the yoga mat and tossed it on the back porch. It was time to set the peaceful lifestyle aside and prepare for adventure. Face tense and brow furrowed, he got down into position and started doing push-ups.

A burnt-orange evening sky glowed over the Amargosa Valley in Nevada when Stetz finally crossed state lines. The last time he visited Area 51 was early in his military career, in the 1980s, back when the F-117 Nighthawk was first tested. He was part of the government oversight team sent by President Ronald Reagan.

Stetz reflected on those wild nights at the base when the Nighthawk resembled a UFO in flight, which meant UFO hunters continuously breached the base's perimeter looking to snap pictures and film video. Those flights edified the long-held urban legend that an alien spaceship crash-landed in Roswell, New Mexico, and two survivors were being housed inside Area 51, where alien technology developed since the 1950's was now being tested.

Military insiders and folks with basic common sense knew the obvious truth: Area 51 was the base where the most highly classified military projects were conceived, developed, and tested by humans and for humans. The isolated location and natural barriers of rock and mountains made it the perfect place to do this work.

In those days, Stetz headed up a military intelligence operation that planted UFO stories in the media as part of a vast cold war psychological warfare effort. If the United States was thought to be in possession of alien technology, enemies would think twice before getting entangled in a war with America. That myth gave rise to places like Daddy

D's Rocket Diner and the Alien Research Center located a few more miles up Highway 95.

Nightfall set in when he arrived at Daddy D's. He had intentionally picked the most touristy spot in the area because it was the best place to have an off-the-record talk. Daddy D's was busy with multiple tour buses in the lot.

Stetz walked in and grabbed a table with a clear view out the window as he waited for his dinner appointment to arrive. The waitress, a middle-aged Mexican woman, approached the table with a menu and a glass of water.

"Only one?" she said.

"No, I'm meeting a friend."

"Can I take your drink order while you wait? We have two margaritas for the price of one now."

"Just a coffee, please."

"I'll be right back."

Stetz heard the thundering sound of a Harley-Davidson roaring into the lot. He watched the rider, dressed in blue jeans and a tucked-in flannel shirt, climb off and remove his helmet. Stetz grinned, happy to see an old friend. He took another sip of his coffee. The front door opened and in strolled Kyle Crist with round glasses on and slicked-back hair. Kyle seemed like a professor who was far from campus, lost.

Seeing Stetz, Crist nodded and walked over to join him at the table.

"Since when did you start riding a Harley?" said Stetz.

Kyle slid down in the seat across from him.

"I picked her up three years ago when I started work out here," said Kyle.

"How do you like it?"

"The work or the bike?"

"Both."

"The work's tedious, but on my rides home I'm free as a bird."

The waitress arrived with a fresh glass of water for Kyle. "Do you need a couple of minutes to look at the menu?" she asked.

"I can order now if you've had time to decide," said Kyle.

"You go first," said Stetz.

"I'll have the tinga burrito with tomatillo sauce and a... one Tecate," said Kyle.

"You know what, that sounds perfect. I'll have the same thing, no beer, some more coffee instead," said Stetz.

She took their menus and walked toward the kitchen.

"How's your mother doing these days?" said Stetz.

Kyle frowned a little. "Oh, I didn't tell you. She passed about six months ago."

"What? I'm so sorry to hear that," said Stetz.

"Yeah, she moved out here to Nevada to be closer to me when I got transferred. She got sick last Christmas and the cold never went away. Turns out she had lung cancer, and after that, she went downhill real fast. It was sad to witness that firsthand. You feel helpless," he said.

"I'm really sorry, Kyle. That had to be rough. Are you doing OK now?" asked Stetz.

"I focus on work all the time to avoid dwelling on it too much."

"I read about the projects you were on before I left Washington, and they made my brain melt. How do you have any kind of social life out here?"

"Vegas," said Kyle with a chuckle.

"So, no strings attached at this time besides your work at the base?" said Stetz.

The waitress arrived with the burritos and set them down. She pulled hot sauce bottles from her apron pockets and placed those in the middle of the table.

"Enjoy," she said.

"No, no strings attached. What's going on? Why are you asking me this?" said Kyle.

"What is the smallest device you've been working on that packs the biggest punch?" said Stetz.

"The J5-MN. Hands down the most lethal of the micro nukes. It leaves a football field-size crater, and it fits in the palm of your hand."

"How volatile is it?" asked Stetz.

"Very stable and secure—until activated. They were originally designed to be used by navy SEALs. One man could take out an entire naval fleet if he placed it under one destroyer."

"Timed detonations, right?"

"Yessir. That's what makes the J5 so dangerous. We're talking a worst-case-scenario device only; that hopefully will never see the light of day."

"We've got a worst-case-scenario moment unfolding, and I need you and your expertise for a job," said Stetz.

"I'm a micro-explosives expert. What kind of job?"

"The kind where you blow things up... on the moon," said Stetz.

Kyle nearly choked on his burrito and coughed before taking a swig of beer and wiping his mouth dry. He leaned forward and whispered, "The freakin' moon?"

"How would the J5 perform on the surface of the moon?" asked Stetz.

Kyle stared at him wide-eyed.

"Under lunar conditions, one J5 would probably leave a huge new crater, visible to the naked eye from Earth. But none of those devices are authorized to leave the base."

"They are now," said Stetz.

"I'm the only engineer who's authorized to handle them. Wherever they go, I go."

"How would you like to do some testing of those bombs up on the lunar surface?" said Stetz.

"You're not messing around, are you?" said Kyle. He took off his glasses and wiped them clean.

Colonel Stetz leaned on the table with both hands folded before him. "We got a heck of a problem up there, and it must be dealt with before it gets out of hand."

"Aliens?"

"Foreign governments claiming lunar real estate illegally," said Stetz.

"And you want to blow them off the moon without a trace of evidence?"

"Bingo. Look—we basically know it's China, and they're trying the same tactic on the moon that they used to construct an airstrip in the middle of the Pacific," said Stetz.

Kyle leaned back and whistled. "This is about control of the highest possible ground."

"That's why we're manning up," said Stetz.

"Wow," said Kyle. He leaned back, thinking. "How long have I been out here, living among the rocks?" he joked.

Stetz chuckled. "You want to get far away from it all for a while? You're the only person who can operate the bombs safely. You're also a damn good medic and a world-class soldier. You check off all of my boxes," said Stetz.

Kyle had a grin on his face. The thought of getting to test some J5's on the lunar surface, far from potentially hurting other human beings, was truly intriguing to his scientific mind.

"Hell, yes, I'm in. When does this all commence? How many bombs are we talking about taking up there?" asked Kyle.

"I'll need you ready to go in one week. You'll be transported to the compound, where you'll live and train for the flight. The president has already authorized the release of six of your bombs for the mission."

"Six! If I detonate one J5 on the moon, people down here are all going know something happened," said Kyle.

Stetz grinned and shrugged. "The news will make something up. You know how the game is played."

THE SHRINKING WORLD

THE CHINESE MILITARY'S first major geopolitical move in the twenty-first century was the clandestine creation of a military base in the middle of the Philippine Sea. The People's Liberation Army (PLA) used its engineering prowess to suck sand from the ocean floor and quickly repurpose it into an island. It started small and ended as a fully functioning armed military base and airstrip. The message was crystal clear—China can build a military presence anywhere on the globe and in record time. What followed was a soft blockade of a major international shipping route. China intentionally threw fuel on an already unfolding escalation of poor relations with the United States and many of its allies. The United States, in return, began sending battleships through the contested waters while performing flyby military recon missions. Each time there was pushback and warnings from the PLA, and each time the United States boldly ignored them. A lot was at stake, but the only ones who knew exactly how much, were the communist leaders in Beijing who plotted the final chapters in what they hoped would become a historic and final blow to America's standing as lone superpower.

Enriched by decades of lopsided trade deals and weak leadership in the West, China's confidence was not unfounded. Armed with hypersonic nuclear missiles capable of striking American bases in Guam, Hawaii, and California, it was obvious, the party leadership decided that the best course of action was an aggressive militaristic one. Taiwan and Hong Kong were ground zero at home, but the recent unveiling of the PLA's first aircraft carriers and stealth fighter jets caught the whole world by surprise.

The technology and know-how needed to construct such equipment were stolen through a sophisticated espionage network that had been infiltrating American universities and industry since the final years of Mao's revolution. These events had set the stage for a conflict that people around the globe sensed was inevitable but very few wanted to happen. Behind every military move is a hidden political ambition. Control of global affairs was suddenly up for grabs; the dragon prepared to strike first. The time was drawing near for the great realignment.

WELCOME TO SPACE CAMP

Sunrise crept into the valley surrounding the Texsat compound. It looked as if a fire were raging over the horizon, it's color spilling from the sky, bringing with it a hot new day.

Inside the spaceship hangar, a team of engineers had been working nonstop for weeks on the TSLM. Scaffolding surrounded most of the body. Wires and cables spilled from every possible opening, connecting the unit to machines and computers on the floor below. The TSLM resembled a sleeker and thicker version of the Apollo spacecraft module—essentially a wide-bodied, almost pyramid-shaped ship with viewports in multiple locations. Texsat engineers, wearing matching white lab suits and gloves, worked as if they were in surgery. The most activity came from the engine bay on the bottom of the ship.

Jim was standing in front of a computer station set on wheels that was lined up against the side of the spaceship. He was indistinguishable from his team, but for the scuffed, dusty orange Texsat baseball cap. Looking at a readout of all systems and their current status, he pressed a button and switched to live video showing two technicians at work in the engine cavity.

"The oxidizer to combustion chamber loop in thruster bay two is still not connecting. Time to chuck it. Don't waste another second," said Jim into his earpiece mic.

The two engineers looked up at the camera that was on them.

"All right. It's coming out," said one of the engineers.

"We need a replacement loop for subthruster six," yelled the engineer.

Jim rubbed his tired face as he activated the hangar doors open from his computer, letting the warm morning air and sunshine flood into the place. The days were blending into one another since he accepted this mission. He swilled the remainder of his coffee. It was time for a refill and time to receive his guests.

After refilling, Jim hopped onto a six-seat golf cart, sipped his coffee, and drove through the open doors. Outside, the morning stillness was broken by the distant fluttering sound of an approaching chopper. It appeared over the horizon as a tiny black dot flying low and fast toward the Texsat compound. Jim recognized it as a government black ops helicopter, and it was arriving right on time, as agreed.

Hector, Kyle, Christine, and Richard wore military backpacks and were strapped into the back of the chopper. They knew each other for all of forty-eight hours before boarding this flight. Richard leaned forward, looked out the front window, making out Texsat in the distance by the launchpad jutting up in the middle. The steel beams reflected sunlight and appeared to glow.

The pilot banked left as he prepared to circle around and land on the nearby helicopter pad. Hector unbuckled himself and slid open the door so they all could see. The rocky, barren dessert was like a dusty, brown version of the surface of the moon.

Christine focused on the arid mountainside in the distance. This was a perfect place to train for the mission, she thought. A few short years ago, she'd never have guessed that a private aerospace company would be hired to send scientists to the moon, including the first female to step foot on the surface. The fact that she is that female, started to hit her hard. Her confident exterior wavered. She snapped out of it as the Black Hawk touched down.

Jim was already parked in front of the helicopter pad. When the rotors slowed some, Richard hopped out, followed by Hector, Kyle, and then Christine. They followed Richard away from the spinning rotors toward Jim. When they were all clear, the chopper pilot saluted Richard and quickly lifted off again.

Jim took another sip of coffee then put it in the cupholder. He stood up and walked over to greet them. The compound's hangars and buildings loomed large behind him, like a small Wild West space theme park, and Jim was Walt Disney himself.

"Welcome to Texsat, everybody," said Jim.

"Great to be with you again, brother. Thanks for all you've done and continue to do," said Richard. "This is Kyle Crist, air force medic; Hector Benevides, special ops medic; and Dr. Christine Uy, NASA lunar mineral scientist."

"Looks like a great team. Very nice to meet you all. Let's hop on the golf cart, and I'll give you a quick tour and show you around," said Jim as they removed their backpacks and tossed them into the back seat.

"Heck of an impressive facility you have here. It's amazing how much you've accomplished with the autonomy you have," said Kyle as he shook Jim's hand.

"Thanks. It's not always this glamorous, but I love it," said Jim.

"Hello. I'm Dr. Christine Uy. You look like you recovered nicely from your accident. What I read about sounded so painful."

Jim smiled. There was something about her that he liked immediately. "Battle wounds. I'm as healed as I'll ever be."

Hector butted in to shake hands with Jim. "Hector. So, when do we see the ship we're going in?" he asked, looking past Jim at the buildings that made up the compound.

"Spaceship hangar is my first stop," said Jim.

Richard sat beside Jim in the front seat. The rest of them climbed in the back.

Jim drove the cart in a circle so that he was facing the spaceship hangar again. A long set of railroad tracks extended from the launchpad and was used to transport the rocket engines and ship before takeoff. He drove along the tracks and as he got closer, the TSLM became visible through the open hangar doors. He pulled up outside and stopped so they could all have a look. It was so much smaller than anyone had anticipated.

"Wait. All six of us are going to the moon in that tiny ship?" asked a very nervous-sounding Hector.

"It's roomy and more comfortable than it appears from down here. The best part is my new engines will get us to the moon in thirty-six hours instead of seventy-two," said Jim.

"Three days locked together in a spaceship. Why did I imagine it took less time?" asked Hector.

"Too many video games," joked Kyle.

"Funny," said Hector.

Jim steered the cart away from the hangar before making his way down a central paved road. A street sign on the corner lamp reads *Superluminal Way*.

"Love the name of this street," said Christine.

"One day I'd like to build a spaceship capable of it," said Jim.

"Science fiction is rapidly becoming science fact," she said.

"What does superluminal mean?" asked Hector.

"Faster than light," said Kyle.

"How long would that take to reach the moon," asked Hector.

"About one second," said Jim.

"Damn," said Hector.

On the left, they passed the modern glass and steel A-frame that was Mission Control. On the right was another building the same size as the spaceship hangar.

"Behind those doors is the engine shop, and we just passed mission control too. We'll head back there later." Jim kept driving and rounded a corner, passing another hangar on the right. "Inside there is the machine shop where my team can manufacture anything we need," he said then slowed the cart down as he neared an intersection. He pointed to a modern-looking log cabin tucked away down the road to his left. "And that was my original office. At one time it was the only thing out here." He turned right and kept going, passing the only corporate-looking building on the lot, located right inside the front gate.

"What do you use the cabin for now?" asked Richard.

"I still work out of it and can sleep there when need be. It's my favorite spot for dreaming and designing," said Jim.

Soon the administrative building was behind them, and they were heading toward a wooded area that backed up against a rocky hillside. Desert pine trees, sky-high, formed a peaceful miniforest out here. A gravel path extended into the woods. As they drove in, sprinklers came to life and began watering the trees and wildflowers.

"I planted this little oasis about ten years ago when I really got into the Japanese concept of forest bathing to clear your mind by being present in nature. Now it's a place for my employees to come think about or discuss the challenges we face. Open sky and no walls are the perfect setting for reflecting and working out complex problems," said Jim.

"You hear that, Richard? We need gardens like this at NASA," said Christine.

"You speak the truth, brother. After combat, all I wanted to do was stare at the trees all day," said Hector.

This section of Texsat property was expansive and very well maintained. More like a Zen garden than something you'd expect to find growing next to a small aerospace company. As they rode around a bend, it was easy to forget they were on a corporate compound. Moments later they came upon a cove that backed up against protruding boulders at the base of the stony hill. There were five luxury Winnebagos parked in a semicircle around a firepit.

Jim pulled over in front of the firepit. "Welcome to

space camp, kids. Each Winnie is exactly the same and fully stocked. All you have to do is pick one and move in."

"You're my kind of guy, Jim," said Hector as he grabbed his backpack and walked over to the first Winnebago on his right.

"You really outdid yourself," said Richard.

"I know a guy with a whole lot full of these. He owed me a favor," said Jim.

Kyle plopped his backpack down on the small couch in the living room area of his camper. He inspected the place he'd be calling home for the next few weeks. There was a TV mounted to a wall, a small desk, a kitchenette, and a shower. He opened the tiny fridge and found it stocked with water, beer, and snacks. "All right," he said.

Richard and Jim were out standing by the firepit when Christine walked out of her camper and strolled up to them, laptop in hand, ready to work.

"These are fantastic accommodations. Is the trip to the moon going to be as comfortable?" said Christine.

"Not at first. We start off feeling like sardines in a can, then fish out of water, then back to the sardine can," Jim warned.

"Still sounds better than cramped and humid DC," she said.

The sound of another golf cart droned toward them. Soon Jance McIntosh and Dale York came around the corner in the cart and stopped.

"Hey team, meet my business partners, Jance McIntosh and Dale York. They run all of my spaceflight operations and will be handling mission control on our trip. I trust these guys with my life, and so can you."

"Don't make me blush," said Jance.

"Without your vision we wouldn't even be in this business," said Dale.

"It's nice to meet you both in person after the phone calls," said Christine.

"Likewise, Dr. Uy. I finished your latest book last night and was surprised to learn that you ran the NASA infrared telescope in Mauna Kea. I want to hear more about that later," said Jance.

"It will be my pleasure."

Dale glanced at his wristwatch. "Time for us to head over to the cabin so we can go over the plan we've worked out for your mission."

"All right everyone—hop on and I'll drive you over," said Jim.

Hector fist-bumped Kyle as he climbed back onto the golf cart.

"Game on," said Hector.

"And we're playing to win," said Kyle.

"We have to," said Jim.

Once everyone was seated, Jim drove around the firepit and down the path that led back to the campus.

Dale had the team sit around a long, rustic wooden dining table in the sunroom of the cabin. A detailed small-scale model of the Texsat rocket with the TSLM on top of it was displayed at the head of the table where Jim was standing. Each seat had an orange folder with a name and number on it as a place setting. Richard smiled when he discovered that his was number two. Windows facing away from the campus toward rolling prairie land were cracked open, letting in the sound of birds. A black metal ceiling fan kept a soft breeze flowing through the place, keeping it peaceful and comfortable.

"Inside each folder you'll find all the information Jim will be going over with you. This folder will not leave the compound, and before you take off, I'll collect and destroy them," said Jance.

They thumbed through the paperwork while Jim started in.

"I want to explain, in broad strokes, the steps we'll be taking during the mission. The reason we have an outstanding record of success here at Texsat is because we prepare extensively for the mission, then execute it. The next two weeks are more about us training you to endure spaceflight and assist me in the event of an emergency," he said before picking up the model of the rocket engine with the TSLM on top.

"Jance, Dale, and I worked out the basic timeline of the mission based on the government's goals and our ship's capabilities, which line up quite well," Jim said while placing the rocket flat on the table.

"Phase one—and, frankly, the most physically demanding—is liftoff and escaping Earth's gravitational pull. This will be the most intense part of the flight by far. It is over pretty fast, but we're going to be pulling nine g's and you'll feel it down in your bones. You might even pass out."

He broke the TSLM off the top of the rocket engine and set the engine part down. He pulled out small retractable flaps around the bottom of the TSLM and then started to slowly twist the capsule like a corkscrew while lifting it higher.

"What's unique about the TSLM design is that after we

reach low earth orbit it has a new way of gaining momentum and saving fuel. No slingshot around Earth is necessary because the perimeter of the module is covered in thrusters that will initiate a corkscrew maneuver until we are clear of Earth's gravitational pull. Then we will use that centrifugal force to accelerate much faster than standard rockets in use today."

"Will there be barf bags included with this flight?" joked Hector.

"Not needed. Once the pinwheel thrusters are initiated, it'll be smooth sailing. The ship's cabin is not connected to the external body—like a washing machine tub," said Jim.

"Absolutely brilliant," said Richard.

"We're going to feel like we're sitting still the whole time?" asked Christine.

"That's right. Meanwhile the ship's external body will be corkscrewing its way to faster and faster speeds," said Jim.

"If I can interrupt for one sec, Jim. How did you come up with the idea for pinwheel propulsion?" asked Kyle.

"Believe it or not, from watching fireworks," said Jim.

"How long have you been using this system?" asked Richard.

"Operation Red Moon will be its maiden flight. But don't worry—every computer model shows it working exactly as planned," said Jim.

A heavy silence settled over them. Nobody expected that answer.

"That's not what we discussed. You said you'd modify what already works," said Richard.

"And I did," said Jim.

"We're flying to the moon in an untested space capsule with an untested spinner engine?" asked Richard.

"Desperate times," said Kyle.

"What are your contingency plans in the event of cata-strophic failure?" asked Richard.

"There isn't one. We're either going to make it or not," said Jim.

"How confident are you in your design integrity?" asked Kyle.

"I'm piloting it, so I'm risking my life with you... and I enjoy being alive," said Jim.

"Oh, good. We have something in common," joked Hector.

Jim lowered the TSLM to the table as if it were landing.

"After what will be a long, boring flight to the moon and we're finally approaching lunar orbit, I'm going to take the module around to the far side and then head south from there. My lunar descent will use those pinwheel thrust-ers again to slow us down. This is where it gets tricky for me—we're going to be landing inside of the Aitken basin, right on the edge of another, even deeper crater called Von Kármán. That is where the foreign boot prints were spotted and where the Chinese have landed an unmanned rover in the past."

"There could very well be more than one Chinese rover up there. All of them will need to be destroyed," said Richard.

"That's your part," said Jim.

"Blasting moon rovers is why I took this job," said Hector.

"Once we're on solid ground, it only takes a few min-utes before I can have you on the lunar surface for phase two. That's when the countdown starts due to limited oxygen supplies in your suits. You'll only have two hours of usable air. Phase two is basin recon and evidence gathering performed by Hector, Kyle, Richard," said Jim, pointing to each man one at a time.

"After you complete your surveillance, we move to phase three—scaling down into the Von Kármán so Dr. Uy can do soil sample collections near the boot print and Hector and Kyle can destroy illegal equipment or structures of any kind."

"So, we're talking about the crater inside the crater now?" asked Hector.

"Yes," said Jim.

"How deep of a climb are we talking about?" asked Kyle.

"A little under half of a mile almost straight down in low gravity, right Christine?" said Jim.

"It could be a little steeper; really depends on where you land," she said.

"All in all, this sounds like it should be pretty straightforward," said Hector.

"There're lots of ways it can spiral out of control. Climbing gear could become locked up or tangled. I'm not certain of the integrity of the moon rock where we'll land... lots of variables to deal with when we arrive," said Christine.

"I considered the existing data and challenged my parts engineers to make a special tool for each of us," said Jim.

Jance handed him a slim wooden case about the size of a backgammon game. Jim unhooked the locks and pulled out a long, shiny silver dagger by the handle and lifted it up. The blade glistened, alien-like.

"A dagger?" asked Richard.

"I call it a moon dagger. Follow me outside for a

moment," said Jim as he led them out the front door and walked down the steps to a gravel path. He found a bowl-ing ball– sized jagged chunk of boulder sticking out of the ground. "Watch this."

He held the dagger by the handle with the blade pointed straight down and barely let it drop onto the boulder. The tip punctured the rock as if it were made of butter and slid halfway in with no effort.

"Whoa," said Richard.

"What the heck did he make that out of?" said Kyle.

"A blend of all the shrapnel from the space junk that hit me, reinforced with titanium," said Jim.

"You made this in-house?" said Hector.

"My metallurgy guy is one of the best. He's an old Comanche tribe weapons- maker, learned the craft from his grandfather. He thought of it after racking his brains on some fail-safe way to make it back up the crater wall in the event that the winch and pulleys fail. Ironically, a super-strong blade that can penetrate moon rock is the ideal survival tool," he said before passing around the dagger to his left and letting each of them stab the rock one time.

"Do not touch that blade with your bare hands," he said.

Richard was the first to inspect it. "So strong, so light. Incredible," he said as he thrust the dagger right into the rock. He let go and left it there for a moment.

"Excalibur!" proclaimed Hector as he pulled the dagger from the stone. He passed it to Kyle next.

"I had my spacesuit team install titanium spikes in our boots at the toes and heels. I already tested them on the mountain rock behind your Winnebagos. You'll be able to climb up manually, like Spider-Man, if the mechanical lifts fail," Jim said.

"How ironic that a primitive tool could save us in a hostile environment we can only reach by futuristic means," said Kyle. He handed the dagger back to Jance, who carefully put it back inside the case while they followed Jim back into the cabin and took their seats.

"Phase three begins once you're at the bottom. Kyle and Hector will head deeper into the crater while Dr. Uy collects soil samples. You're only going to have about one hour to spare down in the Von Kármán, so you have to work quickly. When you're done, I'll attach a climbing line to the winch and help pull you back up the wall one at a time. Once everyone is safely and securely back on board the ship, I can initiate the return flight sequence. The flight home should be smooth all the way up until reentry. After we break through the atmosphere, we're going to pull off a vertical landing about a mile from the launchpad. Any questions?" he said.

"Can I keep that moon dagger after the mission?" joked Hector.

"I'll have it engraved for you."

"Nice," said Hector.

"All right, guys, everything I glossed over is explained to you in detail in your folder. Read and study it nightly. The only test on the material is the live mission," said Jim.

"Next stop is the spacesuit shop. They've already been custom-made to your size, but we need to check for any adjustments that might need to be done," said Dale.

"Great meeting everyone this morning. I have to return to the spaceship hangar for the rest of the day, so I'll reconnect with you guys tonight at dinner. Tomorrow we start training before sunrise," said Jim.

"Thanks so much," said Richard.

"You got it," said Jim.

TRAINING DAYS

AT PRECISELY 4:30 a.m., the team arrived at the spaceship hangar fully dressed in training spacesuits—helmets, climbing boots, moon daggers, and all. Following Jim, they hopped off the golf cart and walked into the spaceship hangar through a set of open double doors.

Jance and Dale had set up a makeshift mission control area beside the TSLM and were seated at the table when the team walked in. They've been up and prepping for this mock run since two in the morning. This marked the official start of what will be long days ahead.

An engineer strolled out of the TSLM and gave Jance the thumbs-up. Another engineer was making final adjustments to a clump of cables under the ship.

"The flight team has arrived," said Dale. He waved to Jim from across the room and gave him the thumbs-up, indicating that all systems were normal. Jim returned the gesture and kept walking toward the ship.

Jim and the team stopped at the bottom of the steps to the TSLM and waited for the engineer to come down the stairs and clear the area.

"All set, boss," said the engineer to Jim as he passed him.

The team started up the stairs and one by one entered the ship for the first time. There was a light hiss and crackle from the built-in communications system in their helmets, which was followed by Jance's voice coming in crystal clear.

"Good morning TSLM team. I hope you all slept and the coyotes didn't keep you up. Go ahead and report in to me one by one for a system check," said Jance into a mic on his desk.

"Team leader, reporting," said Jim.

"Number two, reporting," said Richard.

"Number three, reporting," said Hector.

Number four, reporting," said Kyle.

"Number five, reporting," said Christine.

"Mission control hears you loud and clear. Jim, let me know when you've got everyone settled, and we'll begin the simulation," said Jance.

"Copy," said Jim.

Inside the TSLM, four jump seats were attached to opposite sides of the ship—two on each side—leaving the center clear. Each seat had a white number on the back support, indicating who was supposed to sit there. A short silver ladder in the center led to the cockpit located in the upper nose cone. Storage bays were built into the walls and floor. The cabin was well lit, but its gun-metal gray color cast an intangible pall over the interior.

Jim assisted Christine with her seat to demonstrate to the crew how it worked. He flipped down the sitting portion and guided her to squat into it and lean back. Jim pulled the chest straps across her and attached them into the locks on either side with two loud clicks. She brought down the armrests, by pulling levers on the sides of her head.

"Are you comfortable?" asked Jim.

"More than I anticipated I would be," said Christine.

Click. Click. Click. Hector, Kyle, and Richard all locked into their seats and pulled down the armrests in the same fashion.

"The crew is locked in and secure," said Jim.

"Copy. We're standing by for your engine report," said Jance.

Jim climbed the ladder, disappeared into the nose cone and sat down in the pilot's seat.

The cockpit was designed so Jim could be lying down for takeoff, swivel the chair to a normal sitting position for flight, and also rotate 360 degrees to access the different instrument panels around him. A smaller stationary seat was to his right. A flat screen suspended directly in front of him displayed the TSLM's system statuses in four quadrants. There were two control sticks attached to opposite sides of the pilot seat. Jim toggled through some screen menus and pressed a few commands. "This is the prelaunch engine report on the TSLM. Primary thruster is OK and online. Secondary thruster is OK and online. Pinwheel thrusters are OK and online."

"Copy," said Dale.

"The ship's oxygen levels are optimal, and the reserve supply is full," said Jim as he pressed a few buttons on the screen and the image switched to a digital instrument panel.

Down below, the crew could hear the conversation echo in their helmets. Hector busied himself looking around, zeroing in on all the areas where the ship seemed like it could break apart.

"Initiating countdown sequence," said Jance.

"Brace for liftoff," said Jim. He pressed a button on his screen, and the flight simulator took over. It looked as if they were actually lifting off. The ship's normal live external camera feed had been replaced with video from previous Texsat launches to create the effect.

"Pretty cool," said Hector.

"Only with a lot more shaking," said Richard.

"Releasing alpha rocket boosters," Jim chimed in. After about fifteen minutes of Jim and Jance going back and forth, the screen went blank, and Jim climbed out of the cockpit and down the ladder.

"Welcome to the moon," he said.

"That's it?" said Hector.

"Pretty much," said Jim.

"OK, let's run through it all again. This time I'll throw in some curveballs," said Jance inside their helmets.

"Roger that. Let's go again. I want you up in the cockpit with me, Richard. I'm going to train you to take over in the event that something happens to me," said Jim.

"I thought you'd never ask," said Richard, as he unbuckled himself and followed Jim up into the cockpit. They ran over the flight sequence until lunchtime and then, remaining in training spacesuits, they were transported to the next location by police helicopter.

By the time they reached the top of Monster Rock, located a short distance from Austin, Texas, the sun was out in full force. Dressed up in full spacesuit gear was more than unpleasant. Local police, under orders from the governor, closed all roads for two miles in each direction to keep any citizens from the popular rock-climbing destination for the next few days. Pictures getting out of unofficial astronauts climbing rocks in the midday sun were the last thing the government wanted. The local police were told this was rehearsal for a science fiction movie shooting in Austin in the spring.

Standing at the top of the rocky ridge with roughly 300 feet of stone wall to scale down, Kyle, Hector, Jim, and Christine gathered around Jim as he demonstrated how to install the pulley climbing assist system. Using the moon dagger, he cut a hole as deep as the blade could go into the top of the rock. He took a small winch that was attached to an anchor post and inserted it into the hole. He forced it down with his boot until it couldn't go any deeper, then double-checked that it was secure.

It dawned on him right then and there that he has really been planning for this mission his entire life. From the time when he was a young boy at the tail end of the Apollo era to now, living and working as a successful aerospace engineer and astronaut—his space dreams began with boarding ships to other worlds, and now he was implementing that in real life, relying on old ideas from childhood.

"Once the winch is in good and sturdy, you flip out the pulleys until they lock," said Jim, flipping them out so now it was a short metal T in the ground with one small pulley on each side. "Then you slide one end of the climbing cable through here and the other through here, and then connect that to your belt loop," he said while demonstrating each step. "Now that I'm all hooked up, it's time to rappel down the wall."

Jim sat on the ledge of the rock and lowered himself over as if he were sliding into a swimming pool. He turned his body around and used both hands to begin scaling down.

Richard, Hector, Christine, and Kyle stood overhead as Jim made it look easy.

"Now I'm going to activate my climbing spikes," said Jim, who was now about twenty yards down. He pressed a button located on the wrist of his glove. Three metal spikes released from the bottom tip of both boots. He kicked his leg into the wall and the spikes went right in. This made climbing over difficult spots a simple task. With the stability of the pulley-and-belt system and the ability to gain a solid grip with his feet, Jim could make it to the bottom in record time. When his feet touched ground, he looked up and gave them the thumbs-up.

"That should be even easier to do in low gravity," he said while retracting his metal spikes by pressing another button. Then he activated the pulley system and it began to lift him up the side of the rock. In a matter of minutes, he was gripping the ledge and heaving himself over the top. His spacesuit was a little dusty, but other than that the climbing mechanisms worked perfectly.

"Your turn," he said while dusting himself off.

Jance and Dale assisted the others as they dug out their holes and inserted their pulley systems. One by one they lowered themselves over the ledge and began the descent. Here on Earth, the climbing rig worked as planned and gave the team a sense of confidence about what would arguably be the second most dangerous part of the mission. Christine was the only member of the team who had been mountain climbing before, and it showed in her ability to navigate difficult parts of the stone wall.

"Don't be afraid to use the boot spikes. They are there to make you work less and use less oxygen," said Jim.

Richard thrust his right boot spike into the wall and it got stuck. He glanced over at Kyle. "A little help if you can."

Jim was watching everything from up above. "What happened?"

"My spike is stuck. I can't pull it out," said Richard.

"Wiggle it," said Jim.

Kyle and Hector were moving across the wall toward Richard, so they would be on either side of him. Christine had already set foot on the ground and looked up at the three of them struggling to pry Richard's foot loose.

"Wiggle your foot," said Jim again.

From Christine's vantage point it was like Richard's leg was being electrocuted as he wiggled and pulled it in an attempt to break free from the stone. A moment later his foot was loose, and he went crashing down the side of the rock, ending up head over heels hanging against the wall.

"Oh crap," said Richard.

"How the heck did that happen?" said Kyle.

"His pulley got tangled when he broke free," said Hector as he scrambled down to help Richard again.

Kyle got there first, kicked both of his feet into the rock wall under Richard and stood tall to provide support. "Put your hands on my shoulders," said Kyle.

Richard's weight made Kyle's calves hurt. Hector got to work untangling the pulley wire which was wrapped around one of Richard's legs.

"You got anything to cut this wire with?" asked Hector.

"Use your dagger," said Jim.

Hector unsheathed his moon dagger and with one slice he freed Richard's leg without warning. Richard's feet fell away from the wall, and he tumbled over Kyle while still hanging on to his shoulders. He lost his grip and then started free-falling and was saved only by grasping for and hanging on to Kyle's right foot.

"Whoa!" said Richard.

"This is not how it's supposed to work, is it?" said Kyle as Jim came down the wall using his own pulley and stopped at their level.

"Are you OK?" asked Jim.

"I'm holding steady," said Kyle.

Jim scurried over to Richard and grabbed his shoulder. "You have to stabilize yourself with your boots again."

It was difficult and awkward, but after a few guided kicks at an angle, Richard got one foot locked in.

"I got him now. You can go the rest of the way down and wait for us," said Jim.

Hector and Kyle touched bottom, while Richard climbed down entirely by hand and foot, using the boot spikes and moon dagger to navigate his way. At the bottom, they gathered around Richard and inspected his spacesuit for tears. There were none, but the strain on his leg was real.

"My leg is throbbing. Feels like I got the world's worst rope burn," said Richard.

"How the hell did you manage to get all tangled up?" asked Hector.

"Maybe we don't have to attach the pulley system until we need to go back up," said Kyle.

"Or connect it somewhere else where there's less of a chance of it getting tangled," said Christine.

"The safety harness kept you from crashing all the way to the bottom. Obviously, we have to tweak this a little in the coming trial runs. You'll need to climb up without assistance for now," said Jim.

"I'm OK. I'll handle it," said Richard.

"Is there a way to send the pulley ropes all the way down so they're waiting for us when we reach bottom, and then we don't hook them up until the ride back to the top?" asked Kyle.

"Great idea, but we're wearing them for redundancy. What if we find out the crater wall is too weak and it crumbles under our boot spikes?" said Jim.

"Weak lunar rock or worse—ice covered is very possible," added Christine.

"How much weight would it take to send the pulley rigs straight down the wall?" asked Jim.

"The weight doesn't matter. You could throw a heavy rock over the edge of the Von Kármán and theoretically, it could begin to orbit the moon if you're not careful with your aim," said Christine.

"Use a bow and arrow," said Hector.

Jim cocked his head, wanting more.

"Shoot the wire and belt clips down into the crater with an arrow that sticks into the ground below," he said.

Jim looked at Christine.

"Not a bad idea. A little momentum and weight will keep its trajectory for sure, but with the low gravity and lack of atmosphere to provide friction, the arrow will pick up too much speed and smash into the ground, destroying the belt clips," she said.

"Either way, this is something we need to solve," said Hector.

"I'm grateful it happened here and not when we're stuck in a crater on the moon," said Richard.

"All right let's work it out back at the shop," said Jim.

Christine was the first to lift off the ground. Her pulley dragged her up the side of the rock wall at a steady pace. She used her hands and feet to stabilize herself on the way up. Kyle and Hector trailed right behind her.

Jance helped each of them up and over the ridge at the top, while Dale collected the wires and belt clips. Jim and Richard climbed up manually using a combination of boot spikes and the moon dagger. It was difficult work with the blazing sun beating down on them, but they couldn't resist getting into an unspoken competition to make it to the top first. Jim stabbed and climbed at a steady pace, but Richard's longer arms and legs meant he moved ahead of him quickly.

"This is my second time up," said Jim, picking up the pace, trying to pass Richard.

"Try doing this with a bad rope burn," said Richard.

They were neck and neck to the end, but Jim got his hand up over the top first, glanced back, and smiled at Richard. "Beat ya," he said, huffing and puffing.

"Next… time… ," huffed Richard.

Jance reached down and pulled him up.

Day one kicked everyone's rear, but two weeks filled with relentless and monotonous dry runs of the mission, followed by daily mountain climbing and meditating, made them all strong and healthy in both mind and body.

Each morning began at 03:30 with the team going through every step of the mission in painstaking detail. At the end of each night they met in Jim's cabin and tweaked the plan a little more until the mission was streamlined and simple. Once their training and flight readiness were complete, the final component necessary to launch was out of Jim's hands—the weather. Due to the extreme secrecy of the launch, waiting for the right natural conditions to occur that would provide a layer of cover was a patience game. Each night they went to bed ready.

POWER TRIP

CHRISTINE WROTE IN her journal at the end of every day. Outside her window, a campfire cracked and popped as the sun went down, and the sky turned pinkish-orange with clouds gathering, heading into night. She overheard Hector and Kyle talking in hushed tones, sitting in chairs popping beers by the fire. She hesitated and listened before joining them.

Hector gazed into the fire as sparks danced out and vanished into the night. "We are ready for this, bro. Jimmy's got us all trained to precision."

"I'm looking forward to the three days of rest we'll be getting on the way there, know what I mean?" said Kyle.

Hector chuckled.

"I sure do. Let me ask you something."

"Shoot," said Kyle.

"Are you scared or nervous at all, because I can't read you?"

"A little of both."

"Same. I'm concerned about a spaceship that's never been tested. That right there is why Uncle Sam is paying so much if you ask me."

"You going to be OK?" asked Kyle.

"Oh yeah. I'm committed. I'm being honest. This is all very rushed."

"Aerospace technology is advanced so I'm not worried about the ship. The special cargo we're transporting is another story," said Kyle.

"Don't even joke about that," said Hector.

"I'm not joking," Kyle said while leaning in to whisper his next sentence. "If those explosives blow, we're instant stardust."

"How many were authorized for use?"

"Six. Enough to leave a new crater the size of Los Angeles."

"What kind of explosives do that?" said Christine, standing with her hands on her waist. She grabbed a beer, twisted the cap off, and sat down with them.

"Nobody told you?" asked Kyle.

"Not those details," said Christine.

"How else are we supposed to destroy any equipment we find? With a hammer?" joked Hector.

"I assumed some low-grade explosive, not a nuclear bomb."

"We're bringing micro nukes with us that can be used to blast a new crater to lay the grounds for a lunar base in the future," said Kyle.

"And you're planning to detonate them while we're on the surface? Because that's not a smart idea at all," she said.

"Absolutely not. They're going to be left in a safe box for a return NASA crew after we're back home," said Kyle.

"What if you have to demolish a small structure?" she said.

"I'm carrying low-grade explosives for that job," said Hector.

"Bringing micro nukes to the lunar surface is wrong and unwise," she said.

Richard hopped out of his camper with a beer in hand and joined them. "I'm sorry I didn't let you in on this minor detail sooner, Christine. DOD required it as part of the mission. DOE is counting on you to show us where the best spot for a lunar base should go based on mineral deposits."

"That's no minor detail. What else didn't you tell me?" she said.

"You know everything that I know," said Richard.

"Put me on the official record as opposing this insane idea," she said as Jim and Jance came rolling in on a golf cart for the nightly campfire meeting.

"Noted, and again, I'm sorry you weren't informed. That was my slipup," said Richard. Christine nodded, crossed her arms and sucked up her feelings, overriding personal convictions this one time.

Jim hopped off the cart, grabbed a beer, and joined them. Jance lit a cigar and walked a few feet away to enjoy his smoke.

"Don't drink too many of these tonight. We got some cloud cover moving in, depending on which way it blows it might be showtime," said Jim.

"I talked to the secretary of defense about an hour ago. They've moved three battleships into the Gulf of Mexico to track us," said Richard.

Kyle poured his beer out beside his chair. "Hey, can you toss me a water," he said.

Richard opened the cooler, pulled out a bottle, and tossed him the water.

"Don't waste it." Hector guzzled his beer then twisted open another. "Tell me, now that we've been running perfect missions for days, what's the worst-case scenario in your opinion, not including a spaceship failure?"

"That we end up stuck down in the Von Kármán, and our ride home is up top. It's been keeping me up at night," said Jim.

"If getting stuck is your biggest concern, why aren't you landing right down inside it?" pressed Hector.

"Because only a few probes have ever been down there," said Jim.

"That we know of," blurted Jance from his smoking spot.

"Right. Most of the probes go into the Von Kármán and quickly go off-line or are lost when they attempt to land. China's Chang'e-4 is the only probe to land successfully and report back. So that basin is either extremely treacherous or they already have the place claimed and rigged," said Richard.

"So, it's going to be like landing in the Grand Canyon?" asked Hector.

"More like the rim of the Grand Canyon," said Christine.

"We can't afford to be stranded down there because nobody has a ship that can come rescue us," said Jim.

"How long before NASA's going to catch up to what Jim's doing here?" asked Kyle.

"At a minimum—two years from now for Artemis to get off the ground after initial testing," said Richard.

"What are you going to do with the next two years after you pull this off?" asked Hector.

"Let's make history first. Then I'll decide," said Jim.

They sat around the fire without talking for a moment. The white embers nearing the end of their burn, sparks filled the night when Jim poked the ashes with a stick. A coyote howled in the distance. It was time to turn down and rest up.

Hours later, Christine couldn't fall asleep. She gazed at her mission spacesuit hanging on the back of the bathroom door, boots and helmet on a chair beside it, ready to be put on in short notice.

The sleek suit was custom-made by Texsat and composed of a thick navy-blue material with heavy black stitching. A protective sheath for the dagger was sewn into the right thigh, and a small PDA was embedded in the left wrist. The one-piece suit was much less bulky than anything she'd ever seen at NASA. She focused on the American flag sewn on the left shoulder. The name Smith, the same name that was on every suit, was stitched on the left chest area where a name patch should be.

Soon after, she was out like a light.

OPERATION RED MOON

THE CRESCENT MOON and stars were hidden behind a low cloud cover that crept in overnight. These were perfect conditions. Man-made perfection: military planes had been secretly cloud seeding the sky above Texsat with silver iodide since dusk.

In the months post the Chinese satellite incident, all spacefaring nations were on edge and overly protective of their replacement assets. Working with fresh intelligence data to pinpoint the precise location of each and every object in orbit facilitated identification of the right moment to leave Earth's atmosphere undetected. The best moment had arrived.

The TSLM and rocket engine were moved to the launchpad and prepped for takeoff while everyone slept. Avoiding detection on the ground or during takeoff was helped by the heavy cloud cover, important because keeping the launch shielded in secrecy from recently launched Chinese spy satellites was paramount. Once the ship was in orbit, Jim planned to blend in with existing satellites and space junk before sneaking off toward the moon.

There was a knock at the door. Christine turned over.

"I'm up," she said while fumbling for the light switch beside her bed.

"It's a go," said Jance through the door.

She flicked the light on and sat up, rubbing the sleep from her eyes and stretching her arms. Looking around the small, cramped Winnebago reminded her that she'd soon be stuffed into a small spaceship with four men for thirty-six hours. She stretched again before climbing off the bed, straightening and folding it back into the wall.

She stepped into the small bathroom stall when a scorpion dropped out of the medicine cabinet as she opened it to fetch her toothpaste. "Shoo." She picked it up, opened the bathroom window, and tossed it out into the night. After closing the cabinet, she brushed her teeth before tying her hair up in tight braids that stayed close to her head with clips. At the same time, Hector and Richard were getting dressed in their campers.

Kyle woke up long ago and was already inside the TSLM high atop the launch rocket with Jim. It gave him a rush of pure adrenaline. His face flushed, eyes dancing. It was hard not to have a physical reaction being hours away from riding an untested spaceship's maiden voyage to the moon alongside six of the most destructive bombs ever created.

He gripped the silver metal briefcase tightly in his hand while Jim opened up a compartment on the side wall that was custom-made to transport it. The briefcase fit snugly into the slot; Jim strapped it down inside a metal box which was suspended and kept level by small gyros. Jim closed the door and locked the compartment shut.

"They'll be safe and sound in there. Why do you look nervous?" said Jim.

"I do?" said Kyle.

"Yeah. You look like you saw a ghost."

"If your stabilizers fail and these bombs detonate before we leave Earth's atmosphere, then a sizable portion of Texas and Mexico will be uninhabitable for a very long time."

"I've launched on this rocket beneath our feet over fifty times. I know how reliable my equipment is. You don't have to worry," said Jim.

"I know you've got this," said Kyle.

"You ready for your last hot breakfast?" said Jim.

"I'm starving. Let's go," said Kyle.

Two Texsat engineers boarded the ship to do last-minute checks of the air supply and other environmental systems. A third engineer walked in and climbed up into the cockpit while Jim and Kyle exited across the gantry together toward the elevator.

Kyle stopped in the center for a moment and looked down at the A-frame window of Mission Control and marveled at the activity inside. He took in the view of engineers scurrying, performing final checks and the rocket-fuel trucks pulling away. The energy and buzz of the compound made Kyle proud to be an American, proud to live in a country where a guy like Jim could freely build an aerospace company of his own. And now he was going to have a hand in saving the very nation that created the conditions for its success.

"Are you coming?" said Jim from inside the metal elevator.

"I'm inspired by what we're doing. The adrenalin is pumping big time," said Kyle as the gate closed and the elevator started to descend the side of the launchpad.

"Exploration is in our DNA. When you start to satisfy those cravings to go beyond the bounds is when you feel fully alive. That's why you're so amped up. I'm addicted to that feeling," said Jim.

"I've been making atomic weapons underground for so long that I didn't realize the new space age was really here until I met you."

"It's been here, and the competition is insane. Everyone wants in on space," said Jim.

"Good thing there's a lot of it."

They walked off the elevator, and Jance was waiting with the golf cart to transport them to the breakfast meeting.

The team sat around the table in Jim's office, eating. This was their last cooked meal before for going to the moon, so everyone made the most of it. Not much small talk this morning because it was go time, and there was no turning back. Jim had his spaceship operations manual in front of him, reading over a section. Hector stared blankly ahead as he chewed. Christine wrote notes in her journal.

"All systems still go?" asked Richard, pointing to the operations manual.

"I'm going over a couple of my new safety features that I developed after the crash," said Jim.

"You don't already know it... since you wrote the book?" asked Hector.

"Of course I do. I just don't want to forget," said Jim with a grin.

"I'm grateful we're in this together. It makes up for the mistakes of the past," said Richard.

"You're going to do great," said Jim without looking up

from his manual. He knew they were all getting increasingly nervous, as expected.

Jance plopped down with a tray of hot food and got right into it. "The TSLM is ready. You guys are going to have to board soon. These clouds will begin dissipating in another two and a half hours."

Jim glanced at his wristwatch and then back up at them. "I'll have us off the ground in the next fifty minutes."

Jance pushed back and stood up with his breakfast in hand. "I'll finish this down in mission control. Have a safe trip everybody. Godspeed. We'll be with you on the radio until you reach orbit, then hush-hush time."

"You're the best, Jance," said Richard.

"Thanks for everything," said Christine.

"Make history," said Jance right before the elevator doors closed.

Jim sized up his team, nodding his head in approval. He closed the operations book and slapped the table.

"Well, all right. Let's go find out what's happening on the far side of the moon."

PHASE ONE

Kyle pulled the straps across his chest and locked them into place. The whole time he kept his eyes on the bomb locker in the side wall near Christine's seat. Hector and Richard strapped themselves in at the same time and sat quietly in their seats with helmets on, sealed. No one made a sound.

Jim was in the cockpit, cycling through the ship's systems one last time to make certain everything was online and ready to go. The only difference between now and previous runs was this one was live, with thousands of gallons of rocket fuel pumping below their feet and six massively deadly nuclear bombs beside them in the cabin.

They heard the back and forth between the cockpit and mission control in their headsets.

"Ah… one more check on the fuel gate for me, will ya," said Jance.

"Fuel gate check operation is normal," said Jim.

"Give me the pressure reading inside the oxidizer," said Jance.

"Oxidizer pressure is stable at sixty percent."

"Intertank bay is all green, confirm," said Jance.

"Intertank bay is green."

"TSLM environment is stabilized and normal. That means all systems are go, Cap. We're going quiet now. We'll be monitoring and waiting for your return call. Godspeed and God bless America," said Jance.

There was a moment of weird electrical silence that followed while Jim bowed his head and prayed. He did this before every flight, and this was the first flight since his accident.

He made the sign of the cross when he was finished and then spoke through the helmet communications system. "All right, friends. Hang on to your butts because I'm running this show like I do every job—with a little rock and roll," he said as he pressed the touch screen. "Bad moon Rising" by Creedence Clearwater Revival startled them when it pumped from hidden speakers inside the ship, making everyone chuckle and relax.

Moments later the body of the ship started to vibrate loudly, and nobody was smiling. A deep, scary rumble like sitting on thunder.

Christine gripped her hand rests, squeezing with all her might. "No countdown?" she screamed.

Hector remained stoic and focused. Kyle started to sweat, while Richard looked up at the cockpit and his friend. He could see his backside at an angle that showed Jim's arm move and then the rocket engine increased power significantly.

"Here… we… go," said Jim as he pressed the final button, thrusting the Texsat rocket up into the air. The power was intense and pushed him hard against his seat. Down below, the crew was experiencing significant g's for the first time. Christine's head bobbed loosely atop her neck because she had already passed out.

Team Texsat gathered in front of the Mission Control building, watching the rocket soar into the dark clouds and disappear. A sonic boom came right on time, and it made Jance smile. "They're on to phase two engines now," he said.

The TSLM was still shaking violently as it climbed out of Earth's atmosphere. Kyle exhaled deeply after each of the constant small jolts. He kept his gaze locked on the bomb locker the entire time. Then it felt like they took a giant leap into water, and as if by magic, everything became calm and smooth.

The engines hummed more evenly. Creedence Clearwater Revival was no longer drowned out by the roar of burning fuel. Anyone listening would assume that this spaceship was performing a routine low earth orbit satellite repair job.

Hector exhaled and relaxed his muscles. Kyle too. Richard used one of his long legs to try and wake up Christine by kicking her feet. He could not reach. The ship was surprisingly well insulated from sound, but you could feel the vibrations down in your bones.

Jim was deep into the most difficult part of his job now. His external cameras showed highly detailed video of what he was flying through. He had a total 360-degree view and maneuvered close to an already known defunct satellite in orbit, using the flight sticks on both sides of his seat to roll the spaceship between the satellite and Earth. The TSLM dwarfed the satellite in size, but once he got close enough, they would appear as one item on any radar that was track-ing celestial bodies. Since all of them were cataloged, he could fly invisible until the right time came to pull away.

Jim reached out and pressed a button on the top of the console. Down below, four oval-shaped viewports slid open, providing the crew their first view of Earth from space. There was a sudden and dramatic release of air pressure, and in an instant, everyone felt comfortable. Earth was a stunning sight to behold.

Christine's eyes opened, and she gasped as she realized the Hawaiian Islands dotting the Pacific were directly below them.

Richard was across from her with his finger over his mouth, reminding her to be quiet. Talking was forbidden until they were free of spy satellite range.

Hector and Kyle had a totally different perspective. All they could see was deep space. The black, never-ending nothingness that separates the stars can be humbling when it feels like they're swallowing you whole.

Jim rotated the ship so that they were all facing opposite directions. Now Hector and Kyle could see Earth, while Richard and Christine had the view into deep space.

In the cockpit, Jim kept his focus on maps, waiting for the perfect moment when their orbit brought them across the Gulf of Mexico, across Florida, and over the center of the Atlantic. That's where he planned to turn away and make for the moon, and the moment was approaching fast.

Two minutes after crossing the panhandle, Jim tilted his flight sticks in the direction he wanted to go, pulled the TSLM away from the safety and comfort of Earth's gravitational pull, and gunned it toward the moon for ten long minutes. The ship blasted away at full power, escaping undetected before the rotation of Earth put them in view of the enemy.

Another button ignited the secondary thrusters; then he set the burn timer, checked his critical systems, and flipped two buttons down before lifting off his helmet.

"Y'all can breathe now. We're clear," he said as he flicked his helmet around so that it rotated slowly in front of his face. He attached it to his belt strap, then started down the ladder to the cabin.

"That was absolutely incredible," said Hector.

"Well done," said Christine.

"Where are we?" asked Richard.

"We're pulling away from Earth in a straight line from roughly the area of Key West," said Jim.

"Can we unbuckle out of our seats and experience weightlessness?" asked Kyle.

"Heck yeah. What are you waiting for?" said Jim.

Jim noticed Christine struggling to remove her helmet. He floated over and assisted her. "It should be a smooth ride the rest of the way, but keep this strapped to your belt at all times in case of unexpected gravitational variations."

"I've never felt those before," said Christine, hooking her helmet to her belt. She unbuckled her straps and floated out of her seat with a huge smile on her face, loving every second. "Who hasn't wanted to do this since they were a child?" she said while floating in slow motion across the middle of the ship.

"How long are we going to be weightless?" asked Hector as he flew past her on his back, hands relaxed behind his head. He tumbled in a circle and caught himself at the viewport.

"Zero gravity rules are in effect until the last twenty minutes of the flight," said Jim.

Kyle and Richard removed their helmets and adjusted their seats.

"Can I check out the view from the cabin?" asked Richard.

"Sure thing. Look, don't touch," said Jim.

Richard climbed up into the pilot's seat. He took in the display screens and marveled at the engineering, rubbing his hands gently over the flight sticks and console. "Simply amazing."

Jim popped up behind Richard. He smiled, proud of his ship. "This is what can be done when the government doesn't interfere. This flight would have never left the ground if NASA were in charge, and you know it."

"I know. You're right. Too much regulation kills progress. That's gotta change so we can compete," said Richard.

"So, you're a convert to limited government now?"

"How limited is the question."

"What's it going to take?" asked Jim.

"Bring us home in one piece, and I will join your revolution full stop if you'll have me."

"I'll need experienced help if I want to expand. I'll be thinking about a role for you."

Richard reached out and Jim clasped his hand.

"Thanks, man. Big things in the future. Big things," said Richard as he started to climb back down the ladder after Jim. The rest of the crew was busy floating and looking out the viewport windows. Christine took pictures.

Jim rotated so he was facing the middle again. "We got about thirty-five hours to go. We'll begin our sleeping shifts in one hour, so this is the time I've scheduled to eat."

Christine had her face practically pressed on the window. "Eat again? I'm still full from breakfast," she said.

Hector was doing the same thing on his side of the ship. "Seriously. The anticipation of what the moon is going to be like is literally energizing me."

"And you're going to burn a lot of calories in this environment. You have to try and force yourself to eat and then sleep. One thing we cannot do is arrive on the lunar surface unrested in any way," said Jim.

"You sound like you've been there before," joked Hector.

"He's right. The extreme dryness will suck the energy right out of us, and we'll tire easily," added Christine.

"Let's bust out those delicious and nutritious MREs then," said Hector.

"I need everyone to try and overhydrate. It's going to make your body work better," said Jim as he floated to a silver door against the opposite wall. He opened it and pulled out a box full of NASA-supplied meals ready to eat in plastic bags. Each bag had an attached straw you could suck the food through.

"Which one tastes the least like dog food?" asked Christine.

"They're better than airplane food. You'll be surprised," said Richard as he grabbed one marked *Lasagna*. The crew ate in their seats while Jim floated near the ladder.

"How are you feeling with the hardest part already behind you?" said Kyle.

"Takeoff? That was easy. A little tedious, but routine. Landing in the Aitken basin is my first new challenge," said Jim.

"Maybe we should go over the plan of action once we touch ground one more time, to keep it fresh," said Richard.

"Let's run through it. I land the TSLM, then shut down the core engine, and place the ship on battery power," said Jim.

"Hector and I extend and activate the airlock," said Kyle.

"I power on the external lights and check the seal integrity," said Christine.

"By then you should be lined up and ready to head out. Hector and Richard go first and do recon, while Kyle and I retrieve the J5s," said Jim.

"That is when I'll be laying out the climbing gear and gathering my research equipment for the Von Kármán soil samples," said Christine.

"We should all be geared up and heading to the rim for the climb down by that time. We'll have one hour and thirty minutes to collect the samples and deposit the J5s for the next crew before we must be back on board the TSLM," said Jim.

"We got this locked in. I'm confident that it will go as planned," said Richard.

Jim floated around collecting the empty food containers from each of them. He opened a slot near the food locker and inserted them into a bag with a drawstring. He pulled it tight and closed the door.

"Time to begin sleeping cycles now. Do not forget to keep the helmet on when you're sleeping. Christine, Kyle, and Richard—you guys take the first rest cycle."

"Now I know why every science fiction movie about astronauts shows them hibernating—because of how boring it is out here," said Hector.

"We're flying bare bones is all. If I commercialized this ship, I would install some entertainment options," said Jim.

"Like what?" said Richard.

"Science experiments, games, projects. I can imagine a huge business of flying private citizens to the moon and back in the not too distant future," said Jim.

"Like an airline," said Kyle.

"Exactly," said Jim.

"NASA will be happy to contract out your services again when this is all said and done," said Richard.

"I'm going to dim the lights to make sleeping a little easier," Jim said.

"Where will you be?" said Hector.

"Up in the cockpit keeping an eye on the instrument panels. We can talk on a closed channel, keep each other company," said Jim.

"I need somebody to talk to or I might pass out too," joked Hector. Jim pulled himself up the ladder to his seat and dimmed the lights from his controls. He swiveled into position and eyed the flight system information, taking account of his fuel and oxygen levels first.

For hours the TSLM hummed along beautifully, mostly due to how breathtakingly far commercial aerospace technology had come since the Apollo era. The level of comfort and power achieved with AI-assisted engineering, microcomputers, and building materials that didn't exist until recently almost guaranteed that humankind's future was not limited to one planet. Everyone on board the TSLM realized this truth the moment they set foot on the Texsat compound, but nobody knew it better than Jim. He knew that space was about to become the center of all economic activity, beginning on the moon and then Mars, and reveled in the fact that he was in position to expand well beyond satellite repair.

The hours rolled by without incident; the TSLM's smooth ride felt as if the vessel were standing still back on the ground at Texsat. When the first shift was over, the crew gathered in the cabin to snack, rehydrate, and do light exercise before switching sleep shifts.

Richard moved into the cockpit so Jim could sleep in his seat. Richard was trained and capable of monitoring the system and even taking over the controls in the event that Jim became incapacitated. The emergency autopilot reentry feature that saved Jim last time was also available in a worst-case scenario. No matter where they were in flight, if that button was pushed, the TSLM would begin to automatically return to Earth. The fail-safe was a large black button protected by a red sliding door above the pilot's seat.

Christine used her time to gaze through the viewports and write in her mission journal, a small notepad where she recorded her experiences for a future book. She knew that being the first female on the moon as part of secret mission would be an instant worldwide bestseller when the day came that she could tell the story, so she made sure to keep detailed observations about everything—the interior of the ship, the expressions on her fellow crewmate's faces, the anticipation—she was getting all of it down.

Richard kept quiet up in the cockpit as they droned on through space. The TSLM was more than halfway to the moon. Hector, unable to sleep from the MRE making its way through his digestive tract, fussed to find a comfortable position when a quick flash of light caught his eye through the viewport to his right. Did something break off? Explode? Another quick flash startled him. "Hey, guys? I'm seeing lights outside viewport number two."

"Let me check the camera," said Richard through the cockpit headset.

At first, they didn't hear the strange sounds that were now sweeping over the exterior of the ship. Like the noise of a gentle sandstorm, the swooshing was consistent, getting louder and blending with the persistent hum of the rocket engine.

"Everything reads OK from up here," said Richard in Hector's ear.

"You don't hear that?" asked Hector as he looked over at Christine, who was fast asleep. So were Kyle and Jim. Hector craned his neck as far as he could to peek out the viewport. The whooshing sound grew louder. "What's happening out there?"

"I don't know. All systems are normal," said Richard.

Seconds later a large object rammed the side of the ship and jostled it. And then without warning, another loud slam into the side of the ship. This one woke everyone up. Jim blinked and looked around. Christine was wide-eyed. Kyle didn't realize what was happening and unstrapped himself in a panic.

Another loud slam on the side of the ship knocked it noticeably off course.

"What the heck was that?" said Christine, a little confused.

"Out of my seat!" Jim yelled to Richard as he unstrapped himself and pulled his way up the ladder. Richard came diving down and did a somersault at the bottom when another loud thud hit the opposite side of the ship.

"Fasten your belts and hang on!" said Jim from the cockpit.

Kyle clicked his helmet back on tight as the ship barrel-rolled again.

Richard was the only one who didn't strap down in time. He flopped around the cabin like a rag doll, banging his head so hard on a corner that he blacked out and then floated facedown around the middle ladder.

"Help me! I need help tying him down!" yelled Christine.

Kyle was the closest, so he unhooked himself again, reached out, and grabbed Richard while still gripping his own seat with the other hand. He yanked Richard's body close, forced him into his seat, and pulled the straps.

The ship suddenly flipped forcefully bottom over top, forcing Kyle to hang on to Richard's straps like an acrobat doing a routine. When the motion stopped, Kyle slid back into his own seat and strapped the locks across his chest again.

"You need us to do anything?" asked Hector.

"Hang on," said Jim as the ship rocked and rolled in an uneven, turbulent way that was abnormal for spaceflight.

All eyes were on Richard, blacked out, mouth agape, no helmet. The hammer of objects slamming into the sides of the ship intensified. It was as if the ship was being pelted. Richard's head bobbed furiously like it might snap right off.

"Wake up, Richard!" said Christine.

"Somebody doesn't want us to make it!" said Jim from the cockpit.

The display monitors were chaotic as tiny bits of metal and wire mixed with huge chunks of steel crowded the screen, like flying through a snowstorm.

Jim swooped the ship down, putting intense pressure on the hull, which moaned like an old wooden sea vessel in a storm, as if the walls might blow apart at any moment. He knew gravity could hold the shrapnel storm up only to a limited diameter and that if he forced the TSLM in a straight line, he would soon pass through to the other side. Determined to escape the mess alive a second time, his reflexes and maneuvers clicked into overdrive as he prayed under his breath all the way through the storm.

Minutes later, they were out and in the clear again.

"Holy cow," said Kyle.

"I thought we were all dead for sure," said Christine.

"Are we all clear?" said Hector.

"We're clear but took on some damage," said Jim.

Kyle unbuckled himself and checked Richard's vitals.

"He's passed out," said Kyle as he gently slapped Richard across the cheeks. He dug around in the leg pocket with a red cross on it and pulled out a smelling salt pack, crushed it in the palm of his hand to activate the salt, and then held it under Richard's nose. "Time to wake up, buddy. There he is."

Richard's eyes fluttered opened, momentarily groggy and incoherent as he came to. "What's going on?" he mumbled.

"Everything's OK. You got knocked out, but you're going to be fine. The ship is fine. We're all doing fine," said Kyle.

"Except for the fact that somebody might know we're coming," said Jim as he pulled himself down the ladder with a concerned look on his face.

"What is that much shrapnel doing this far out?" said Christine.

"Was that junk from the same storm you got caught up in?" asked Hector.

"No way. My accident happened close to Earth. This is too far out for space junk. It was scattered out here for a reason," said Jim.

"Maybe that shrapnel is from some other wreckage that wasn't reported," said Kyle.

"Or wreckage that somehow drifted out this way," said Hector.

"We were rammed by a probe. I watched it fly away," said Jim.

"Are we heading right into a trap?" asked Christine.

All eyes were on Richard, who massaged his neck with both hands. He had come to and was the only man on board who might have insider intel.

"Nobody knows," said Richard.

"We're a few hours away from entering lunar orbit so be ready for more surprises. I have to remain in the cockpit for the rest of the flight. Stay alert down here," said Jim.

"What can we do if the ship gets attacked by a missile?" asked Hector.

"Do you pray?" said Jim.

"I do now," said Hector.

"Then pray hard that we make it to phase two in one piece," said Jim ominously, turning around and pulling himself up the ladder to the cockpit.

Hours later the TSLM crossed behind the far side of the moon without incident, disappearing into total blackness. Descent and landing were where the mission had the biggest chance of catastrophic failure; Jim made sure that he was ready for the worst. He had the flight system running on manual control, which required him to turn on and off every engine and stabilizer by hand. Many of the external cameras used for radar mapping were destroyed in the probe attack, forcing him to pilot the ship by instrument panel and gut alone. The risk of flying right into the side wall of the basin and never being heard from again was high; Jim composed himself to prevent his nervousness from worrying the crew. After making it this far, he was determined to land successfully and step foot on the surface of the moon—a dream that he'd been chasing since childhood.

Down below, the crew sat in stone-faced silence as the uncertainty set in, the only sound the engine's light hum. Visibility was minimal through the viewports. The fuzzy glow from the computer systems provided the dimmest of light inside the ship. Jim edged the TSLM closer and closer to the lunar surface.

"A couple more minutes," said Jim as the ship shifted and cranked. Weird, unnerving sounds popped off on different sides of the cabin. Tiny rocket engines fired with short flashes of light, revealing through the viewports a wall of moon rock that was too close for comfort.

"Oh God," said Christine as she caught a glimpse.

Another engine fired, lighting up the view, which was like looking down into a dark and colorless canyon—deep chasms of layered moon rock awaiting their death. The TSLM started to rotate until it was rocketing sideways at 2,500 MPH about two miles above the surface. Jim killed the thrusting engines and began rapid controlled descent.

"I'm bringing her down now. Only a couple more seconds and we should be on the ground. Brace," said Jim.

The ship lurched toward the surface in a series of rapid-fire engine blasts. It rocked from side to side, then leveled off like a falling leaf. Jim was sweating hard, hand-firing the engines for the last five hundred meters. The sensors showed him how close he was to the surface: three hundred feet… one hundred feet. Another slight rocking of the ship, then awkwardly but not perfectly straight, he touched down on the surface of the moon. There was a moment of stunned silence and then, "Touchdown, baby! America is back on the moon!"

"Hell yes we are!" said Hector.

"Great job landing, my friend. Very intense last few moments but you handled it perfectly," said Richard.

"Amen," said Christine.

"Now comes the fun part," said Kyle.

Jim shut down all systems except for life support and then climbed down the center ladder of the ship. While the others unstrapped themselves, he walked to the door, cupped his hands at the viewport, and peered at the pitch-black exterior.

"Smooth work, Captain," said Christine.

"You flew up here and landed like a boss," echoed Hector.

"We came pretty close to dying on descent," said Jim, face still pressed against the porthole. He turned around, facing Richard. "Let's hope we've landed somewhere close to the right spot. The basin is too vast for us to go wandering far, and I don't have enough rocket fuel for anything more than one takeoff."

"Understood," said Richard.

Hector and Kyle opened a locked panel on the wall. Kyle unhooked five different clamps and then closed the panel again. Next to the panel was a crank like you would find on a bay window. Hector folded it out and turned the crank until the airlock was fully extended.

"Airlock extension locked and ready," said Hector.

"Copy," said Jim as he moved to the airlock door. One by one, they gathered around him to peer out of the windows, but there was still nothing but darkness.

"And the Lord said, 'Let there be light,'" said Jim before he flipped a switch. Floodlights turned on and created a ring of clean white light all around the TSLM. They could finally observe the lunar surface up close.

"Whoa. So beautiful. Look at that texture," said Christine.

"Is that snow?" said Hector.

"It is. Incredible. You landed right on a permafrost deposit," said Christine.

"I searched for someplace level," said Jim.

Hector studied the gray, dusty surface, which reminded him of windswept talcum powder. It was mostly smooth, except for a few ripples and clumps of moon rock scattered about that glittered in the floodlights where the icy snow crystals mixed in.

"So, there *is* water on the moon," said Hector.

"Lots of it, mostly trapped under the surface," said Christine.

"Now that I'm seeing this place in real life, why is it so important?" said Hector.

"It's what you don't see," said Christine.

"Like?"

"Extremely rare minerals we don't even have on Earth," she said while closing her helmet and making sure it was sealed shut.

"Comm check: Does everyone hear me?" asked Jim.

"Roger," said Hector.

"Loud and clear," said Christine.

"All good," said Richard.

"Copy," said Kyle as he unlocked the compartment that held the J5s. He pulled the briefcase out and opened it, revealing two liter-size metal tubes. He inserted them into a special holder on both sides of his belt.

"You did say those are stable, right?" said Christine.

"Nothing to worry about. Even if I dropped them off the side of the cliff," said Kyle.

"How are they armed?" she said.

"Timer that has to be set by code," he said.

"Remember, we have to stay within a half mile of each other to use the communications system. It could be very easy to jump too far away in our excitement and become cut off," said Jim.

"The oxygen clock is ticking," said Richard.

"Right. I need everyone to stay back while I activate the airlock for opening," said Jim as he flipped open a new side panel and pressed a blue button that initiated an oxygen transfer from the inside of the ship to the airlock. Once it was stabilized, a green light blinked on above the door.

The cabin was tightly cramped as they stood ready to exit, back to chest. Jim closed the door on the small control panel and flipped a series of switches above his head. The lighting inside turned off except for beads of light that outlined the exit and windows. The outside lights stayed on and kept the place bright enough to see one another.

"Christine, you go first," said Jim.

"Why me?" she said.

"Because you're the first woman to ever be up here, and

you deserve the honor. I wouldn't have it any other way," said Jim.

"Yeah, step out there, Dr. Uy," said Hector as he slid back so she could be in front.

"Chivalry in space? I like it," she said.

"Time to make history, Christine," said Jim. They all moved aside as she shimmied her way to the airlock door.

"I'll be right behind you," said Hector.

Jim pressed the wall button that opened the airlock door. Christine stepped into it and unzipped the entrance to the other chamber. She stepped through and zipped it back up. The whole time the airlock stayed inflated like a balloon.

"After you open the door, go ahead and kick the ramp down with your foot," said Jim.

"Copy," said Christine. She pressed the button that opened the door to the vast gray and barren plain of the lunar surface. One kick of the ramp made it flip over and land on the ground. She took one small step at a time down the ramp until she was one foot away from the surface.

"That's one small step for man, one giant leap for women," she said while hopping as high as she could off the ramp and onto the moon. She fell forward with a tumble and off-balance hop, laughing all the way.

"Be careful, Dr. Uy," said Richard.

"This is nothing like I expected," she said, stopping her fall with the palms of her hands.

"How does it feel to be out there finally?" said Richard.

"Hard to describe—surreal and inspiring, but mostly surreal," said Christine.

The airlock door opened, and Hector was on the ramp,

walking down. He squatted and jumped off the ramp, soaring five feet into the air before coming down, feet kicking wildly, landing with a thud. He got up and turned around, smiling wide through his helmet. "This place rocks."

Kyle stepped out careful and slow, then bounded over to Hector's side, followed by Richard and Jim. For a moment they all took in the surroundings. The jagged rocks and ice drifts contrasted with a black star-filled cosmos.

"It sure is peaceful up here," said Christine.

"Dr. Uy, can you determine which direction the Von Kármán crater is?" said Richard.

Christine flipped back the cover on her wrist PDA. It was a small basic tablet preloaded with critical information, which was wrapped into her suit. Her right glove had rubber points that allowed her to tap the screen effortlessly. She pulled up a program that linked up to the ship's location information. After processing it, a map came up with her exact location pinpointed on the screen.

"Wow. We're less than a half mile from the Von Kármán crater," she said.

"Damn solid landing," said Richard while patting Jim on the back.

A red flame of light shot straight up from the darkness in the Von Kármán. Christine was the only one facing it. She pointed.

"What is that?" she said.

The four of them turned around and watched the long, thin afterburner of some kind of rocket that was rapidly accelerating out of a crater before banking away from their location.

"Kill the TSLM lights," yelled Kyle.

Jim was already fumbling with his wrist computer. Frustrated, he dove back to the ship and killed the lights by punching a master switch beside the airlock door, leaving them in the safety of total blackness.

"That's a probe. What the hell is going on up here?" said Richard.

"That probe is similar in size to the object that attacked us on approach," said Jim.

"Do you think it saw us?" said Christine.

"Let's hope not; we're sitting ducks up here," muttered Hector.

They huddled beside the ship and waited as the small rocket curved up and away from them. It seemed to fly away as if it were leaving the moon.

"We have to climb fast to the bottom of the Von Kármán and find out where that rocket launched from," said Richard.

"You think they have some kind of a base down there?" said Kyle.

"We're here to find out," said Hector as he flipped down his night vision binoculars. The probe was now a speck that blended in with the rest of the stars in space, so they started to make their way toward the Von Kármán crater rim a half mile away. It was a slow, awkward walk across powdery sand and crunchy ice that made it seem like they were trekking across the remotest corner of Antarctica. Ten minutes into the trek, Hector noticed a pole sticking out of the lunar surface near the crater's ledge.

"Do any of you guys see... that stick to my east?" said Hector.

"No, where?" said Jim.

"I see nothing," said Richard.

"Where are you looking?" said Kyle.

"To the far right of us. I swear. It's like a pole or something. Hold up. I'm switching to binoculars," he said.

"Is that... a flag on a pole?" said Jim as they all trailed Hector.

"It sure is," said Hector, who moved to the left, revealing the five-starred red flag of China attached to a metal post exactly like the American flag planted in Tranquility Base on the opposite side of the moon.

"I guess we know who's up here," said Jim.

"Step aside. I have to document this," said Richard. He lined up his helmet with the flag and used the built-in camera to capture the image.

"I'm not surprised at all," said Kyle.

Hector drew his moon dagger out and cut the flag down. He crumpled it in his hand and stuffed it into a leg pocket before starting back toward the crater rim. "Time to go pay our friends a visit."

THE VON KÁRMÁN CRATER

MINUTES LATER THEY reached the edge of the Von Kármán crater. The view from here reminded Hector of looking down into a valley from atop a rocky cliff in Arizona—if everything were in black and white.

"Would you look at that? A whole instillation is down there," said Richard.

"Crazy. I can make out four, no five silos that surround a dome-like building," said Kyle.

"The communists have a functioning lunar base already? When did this even happen?" said Jim.

"You expect us to believe that not one person knew this was up here?" said Hector.

"Notice how all of the structures are covered with and blend in with lunar dust? That's pretty good camouflage from satellites." said Christine, disappointed in herself, that she missed this large a finding despite hours of meticulous research. "I study the moon and didn't catch any of the clues until the boot print."

"A crater within a crater, creates shadows as well. It's a smart location for a secret base you don't want found." said Jim.

"Maybe our satellite was hacked," said Richard.

"What do you mean?" said Christine.

"Maybe you received pictures from a lunar satellite that were old pictures and not the actual photos," said Jim.

"Until the one slipped through that had the new boot print, which triggered the destruction of our communications satellites," she said.

"Don't lie, Richard. Did you know this was up here?" said Jim.

"Absolutely not. We only knew that it was a possibility, and now that it's a reality, we are going to have to change the plan and use those J5s to destroy those buildings. The Chinese are in extreme violation of the 1967 Outer Space Treaty, and this is now an enforcement job," said Richard.

As angry as Christine was, the science intrigued her. "What if they're doing incredible research? Something all of humankind can benefit from?" said Christine.

"That's what you're going to tell me when we're close enough to examine the place for ourselves," said Richard.

"We don't have enough oxygen to go that far and back," said Jim.

"We have to move fast," said Richard.

"You know better. Breathing heavy will use your supply up even quicker," said Jim.

"How far away is it?" asked Kyle.

Hector stood still, taking a reading with his built-in electronic binoculars.

"An extra three-quarters of a mile from the bottom of this ridge," said Hector.

"We won't have a moment to spare if we make it to the

silos and back. That means zero time for stopping to look around," said Jim.

"Unless we can breach the base and find oxygen inside," said Richard.

"It's possible by the looks of it. I can make out tire tracks going around the left side of the closest silo," said Hector.

"What do you think its function is, Christine?" said Jim.

Christine focused her binoculars in the direction of Hector's gaze. The tire tracks were too deep and too wide to be crew transport vehicles. "Oh, that's gotta be a mine," she said without a second thought.

They had gone over the crater descent plan so many times back on Earth. Almost in unison, the team had their climbing gear out and attached to their suits and were ready to make the descent.

"One half-mile down. Be safe but move as fast as you can," said Jim.

"All right. Let's do it," said Hector, anxious to climb down.

Christine pulled a handheld scanner out of her left side pocket and strapped it to her right forearm. "Initiating ground stability check," she said before hop-walking a little closer to the edge. She pointed the small remote control-size device at the ground, and a white beam of light shot down and waved back and forth and up and down across the surface. She glanced back and forth from the ground and the screen on her scanner. After a moment, she stopped and drew a circle on the surface.

"Here's anchor spot A. Solid moon rock. Will hold," she said before hop-walking along the ridge a few feet over. She performed the same ground check and marked the area.

She did this over and over until there were five spots within reach, so they could climb down like window cleaners on a skyscraper.

Jim and Richard worked the hand crank drill that bored down into the moon rock. It was a T-shaped device with teeth that held as it was screwed in deeper.

"A little… more… ," grunted Richard, applying all his weight to the handle. Jim pulled back on the other side. Now a metal T with two loops at the top stuck out of the rock.

"This is deep enough," said Jim. "I'll rig the motor while you start on the next one."

Richard hopped away. Jim had developed tiny motors that he used to tow satellites to his spaceships for repair. The small handheld device that he was fitting to the metal T had the capacity to pull a one-ton weight. The ability to move up and out of the crater quickly was critical to the mission now more than ever.

Kyle was the first to sit his rear down on the ledge of the crater and dangle his heavy feet over. His metal belt loops were taut with a thin silver wire running through them that looped back to the metal T in the ground. Wrapped around his left hand was a controller that also was connected to the loop via wire. The trick here was for him to scoot forward, free-fall long enough to position his entire body against the wall, then use the pulley motor to stop. From there he would turn around and use his climbing shoes to dig in and guide his climb down.

"We're playing ready-jump out here. When you're ready, you jump," said Jim.

Kyle scooted forward and slid over the edge in what

seemed like slow motion. As his back skimmed the crater wall, he used the device to slow himself down. Once suspended and stable, he turned around and kicked his front spikes into the moon rock.

"That worked perfectly," said Kyle as Hector came sliding down next to him.

"Last one down is a rotten egg," said Hector as he released his pulley break and started descending too quickly. He had to use both hands and feet to slow and stop himself.

Slowly, painstakingly, inch by inch they scaled down the face of the crater. There were clear areas and areas that required some lateral moves. All in all, it was smoother than anticipated and softer too. Their boot spikes and handgrips penetrated the rock easily. With each downward movement, the pulley system unwound more silver wire.

"How are we doing on time?" said Hector.

"Right on schedule, and we're about halfway down," said Jim.

"This is much easier than I thought it would be," said Christine.

"Speak for yourself. My legs are already tired and sore," said Richard.

"Kick in lighter. You're killing it every time, and you don't need to," said Jim.

Richard looked down and realized that his spikes were in twice as deep as Jim's, a few yards away. Jim easily pulled his out and lowered himself again before another light front kick to stop. Richard pulled out his left foot, then started to work his right. He got it out and began the slow, pulley-assisted descent to his next kick and stop. When he was level with Jim, he kicked into the wall lighter than usual and came to a full stop.

"OK, you're right," said Richard.

"We're all learning as we go," said Kyle.

Christine slid down beside them. She had incredible balance. "One day when cities are up here, this will be a tourist spot for sure. moon rock climbing is too much of a thrill. And would you take a look at that view?" she said while leaning back and extending her arm toward the eerie fog of deep space, riddled with stars and distant flickers of light.

"I feel small as an ant," said Jim.

"Makes me wonder what else is out there. We can't be the only ones," said Hector.

"The probability of us humans being the only intelligent life in the universe is a negative number. I never believed we are alone," said Christine.

"We are the aliens," said Jim as they worked their boots loose and continued down. There was no warning, no sound, as Kyle's support wire snapped, and he began to free-fall away from the crater wall and the group.

"Kyle!" yelled Hector.

"No!" Christine cried.

Kyle was falling in lower gravity than on Earth and knew that if he could kick or grab anything, he could slow himself down before hitting bottom. The crater slope was steep and smooth. He clawed and scratched while frantically trying to kick his spikes into the passing moon rock. One moment he was upside down; the next he was head up. The pulley got tangled around his left arm and started cutting off circulation. His body smacked hard against a sharp rock ledge and tore a small gash in his suit right below the area where the wire was knotted around his arm.

The rest of the crew could only watch, horrified, as the fall took place in total silence and what looked like slow motion. Like a rock skipping across the water, Kyle bumped off the crater wall, fell, bumped again, until he finally hit bottom with a bone- breaking thud. He lay there motionless, still breathing. Dazed, he moved both hands to the J5s connected to his belt, checking that the micro nukes were not lost in the tumble.

"Kyle, say something!" said Hector.

They heard his heavy breathing and faint grunting sound. He was definitely alive.

"Sounds like he had the wind knocked right out of him. I hope nothing's broken," said Hector.

"It will be a miracle if nothing is broken. Remember, there's no atmosphere to create friction so he picked up speed on the way down," said Christine.

"I'm going to scale down faster," said Jim.

"Don't risk it. You're the only one who can fly us home," said Richard.

"I got him," proclaimed Hector. He then unhooked his boot spikes and started a controlled rapid descent down the crater wall. "Hang on, buddy. I'm coming for you."

Jim looked at Richard and Christine. "His suit is leaking. I can see it from here."

"Did anyone catch how he fell?" said Richard.

"I didn't, but if those silos are part of a base, then we need to seek help in there before he dies," said Christine.

"Christine. Let me remind you that we're here to blow

those silos off the face of the moon, not to make friends," said Richard.

"This is not what I signed up for," said Christine.

"The situation has changed," said Richard.

"I know. Kyle is lying on the bottom of a crater with a hole in his spacesuit," she said while kicking off and starting her descent again.

"Hector's got him," said Jim.

With deliberate controlled movements, they bounced off the crater wall and then repeated the step when they hit the wall again, looking like man-frogs leaping backward down a slope, but it worked.

"Let me have an update, Hec," said Jim.

"He's alive and the pulley wire created a tourniquet above where his suit was ripped," said Hector.

Hector examined Kyle's half-opened eyes. He was in pain and having difficulty breathing. "Don't worry, brother, I got you." Hector pulled back a patch on the inner thigh area of Kyle's suit and found a small port. He opened the medic bag on the side pocket and pulled a thin orange tube from it and plugged it into the port. "Let's take that pain out of the way. Needle going in," said Hector.

"Hec... my ribs... feel broken," said Kyle through clenched teeth.

"Inhale slowly while the pain meds kick in," said Hector, working quickly with the suit-patching kit from inside his shoulder pocket. The material adhered to the suit like duct tape but thicker.

"Gotta hand it to you, Jim. The government is never this prepared for every occasion," said Richard.

"I was the kid who took the Boy Scout motto to

heart," joked Jim as he made it down and hopped over to assist Hector.

Christine kneeled on the opposite side of Hector. Richard stood over them near Kyle's boots.

"He needs real medical care," said Christine.

"What's your assessment?" said Richard.

"He's going to make it, but we have to bring him inside somewhere and take a closer look," said Hector.

"It's best we take him back to the TSLM." said Jim.

"The base is closer now. If any people are up here, there will be a medical bay of some kind. I say we break in, lay those bombs and run," said Richard.

"Not until we treat Kyle," said Jim.

"I second that," said Christine.

Richard looked at Hector to seek an ally to his side.

Hector shook his head at Richard. "The mission will be completed, but my brother's life comes first," said Hector.

"All right, so we agree. We're going to try and enter the base and patch Kyle up; then we're laying the J5s and heading back to the ship without being discovered." said Richard.

"Stay the course." grunted Kyle.

"Time is oxygen. Let's get moving." said Jim.

THE DOME

HECTOR AND JIM pulled Kyle using the broken pulley wire to create a handle between his boots. Richard led the way toward the mysterious base about a quarter of a mile away, stopping to take pictures of the base with his helmet camera. Having no idea if they were being monitored and no choice but to trek across the open crater floor, everyone was on edge. The only light came from a faint glow coming from the central dome of the lunar base. Everything else was shrouded in darkness and covered in dust.

"How are you hanging in there, buddy?" said Hector back to Kyle.

"I'm feeling pretty normal again. What did you give me?" said Kyle.

"A touch of fentanyl to get you pain-free until I can check for internal bleeding," said Hector.

"I landed pretty hard. I hope nothing is ruptured," said Kyle.

"Your vitals are stable now. Some broken bones is my guess," said Hector.

Christine stopped walking and kneeled. She rubbed her gloved hand in the soft, powderlike moondust. It sparkled.

"Guys, this dust… is not natural," she said.

"In what way?" asked Richard.

"It's too fine, too powdery, and has some kind of crystal sediment mixed in with it."

"Like a manufacturing byproduct?" asked Jim.

"Yes. Processed. Keep walking, I have to take a small sample. I'll catch up."

They kept walking while Christine pulled a white tube from one of her shoulder sleeves. She scooped some of the moondust inside and closed the lid. She kept it in her hand, shaking it while standing up and walking again. She then opened her hand and the middle of the tube had a triple black line around the center now.

"Richard. This is waste from that processing plant and it's testing positive. There must be a chimney stack that shoots this byproduct out and it falls down here," said Christine. She stood up and hopped forward to catch up.

"What are they producing that they gotta be this far from Earth?" asked Hector.

"It's ^{3}He—formally known as helium-3, it can only be found in large quantities up here and happens to be the lone missing ingredient needed to create clean fusion energy. If the Chinese are mining and processing H3, that means they're on the verge of creating a new energy source that would mean the end of fossil fuels," said Christine.

"No wonder they sent us up here with fireworks," said Hector.

"Whoever controls the energy of the future controls the future, and we're not going to let it be controlled by the Communist Party of China," said Richard.

"But do we have to destroy it? If this base is an

operational H3 mine, we need to know how they're doing it," said Christine.

"How much H3 does it take to make fusion energy?" asked Jim.

"One gram could power New York City for over fifty years," she said.

"So, a very small amount would be priceless—especially if you're the only ones who have it," said Hector.

"And we're here to make sure that monopoly doesn't happen. No nation is allowed to come and claim lunar land for themselves and dig a mine," said Richard.

"What a shame that we're here to destroy something that might be beneficial for the planet," said Christine.

"Whose side are you on?" huffed Hector.

"The side of reason," she said.

"I agree with her. We don't have to go in with guns blazing," said Jim.

"We were sent here to do a job and we're going to do it," said Richard.

"Why, so your political ambitions back home will be more successful?"

"I resent that, Jim. The last thing I want to do is have to fight, but if it comes down to combat, so be it."

Christine made eye contact with Jim, thankful for the backup. They were about one-tenth of a mile away from the silos when a trap door slid open on top of the closest one. A wide-mouthed cannon made of metal emerged. With no sound at all, fine moondust came shooting out of the cannon at an incredible volume and made it look like it was snowing around the base. The moondust floated around and created near-whiteout conditions that approached them like a sandstorm.

"This gives us great cover to find the entrance without being seen," said Jim.

"You still hanging in there, buddy?" Hector said again looking down at Kyle.

"I'm here and listening," said Kyle.

"How long do you think it will take the dust to settle, Christine?" asked Richard.

"Estimating based on the conditions, it will all fall to the ground in about thirty minutes or less in this gravity," she said as the cloud of dust thickened around them.

The probe that had launched moments after they landed appeared on the horizon behind them like a speck of moving light. Completing an orbit of the moon, the small afterburners were thrusting it slowly into position as it neared the silo base ahead of them.

"Try to stay hidden in the cloud," said Jim.

"Lie down. We can't be spotted," said Richard.

They moved into the dusty cloud, stopped walking and kneeled around Kyle. It was difficult to focus on anything more than three feet away, so they were likely invisible from above.

"That probe is landing in this mess—it must be a remote-controlled drone," said Jim.

"The question is no longer are there people up here, but how many are we going to face," added Hector.

"From what I made out when we were on top of the crater, the probe touched down on a landing zone on the far side of the base from our current position," said Richard.

They were a few yards from the nearest silo now and

moved as a group up behind it. It was four stories tall and wide enough to provide cover. There were no markings or openings in plain sight.

"Who's coming with me to find an entrance?" Hector asked.

"I am," said Jim.

"If something happens to you, nobody is getting home. You should stay back with Christine and Kyle," said Richard.

"We're already way off script and I don't trust you right now. Stay put," said Jim as he and Hector hop-walked around the silo, toward the central dome. It was the obvious place to look for humans and shelter.

The closer they got, the more details they could take in. The dome's circumference was about the same as a standard running track. Well-developed pathways with enough space for vehicles stretched from four opposite points. Two of them led to small launchpads where the probe had returned. It was all visible from their new vantage point and revealed a level of engineering sophistication that shocked Jim.

"This is not looking pretty at all. We might be in for a fight. You ready?" said Hector.

"I'm not up here to be captured," said Jim.

"I see an entrance straight ahead and to the right. Look at the size of those doors," said Hector. They hopped down to the entrance and stood looking up at the two massive doors that were almost as tall as the dome itself.

"How the heck did they build all of this?' said Hector.

"We may have already lost the future," said Jim.

Jim spotted a control box on the right side and moved to it. "Over here," he said as he inspected the control box.

It was locked shut, covered in Mandarin hanzi writing. Instructions or warnings, they didn't know.

"We need you down here Christine, to read the controls," said Jim.

"On my way."

"What about Kyle?" said Richard.

"I don't want him to get caught red-handed. Stay back with him until we breach the base," said Jim.

Christine hopped next to Jim who now had had the control box open. There were a series of switches each labeled in Mandarin. Colorful, confusing. It seemed like too many options for a simple lock.

"You understand any of this?" asked Jim.

She inspected the control panel and didn't hesitate to press an orange square-shaped button. The tall doors jolted slightly then stopped.

"Whoops. Forgot to press unlock first," she said while pressing a blue circle-shaped button followed by the orange square again. This time the doors slowly started to fan out and open up.

"We're in, move down here, Richard," said Hector. Seconds later Richard came toward the door with his pistol in one hand and Kyle's boot handle dragging Kyle in the other. Kyle aimed his pistol straight ahead with both hands while he was pulled. Jim, Hector, and Christine took up positions on opposite sides of the door with their weapons drawn, waiting to see what was on the other side.

The doors stopped when they were wide open. Jim walked around the door and peeked inside the cavernous dome, not believing his eyes. The red nose cone of a tall missile poked up above the gantry of a launchpad in the center of the dome. It was marked with the nuclear symbol and more Mandarin on the side. An ominous and dramatic sight considering the implications.

"Some of us aren't getting out of here alive," said Hector.

"They've got bigger guns than we do," said Jim.

"I'll be damned," said Richard, taking multiple pictures with his helmet cam.

"What is a nuclear missile on a launchpad doing on the moon," said Kyle, who knew better than anyone else what he was looking at.

"Let's move inside and find a place to hide, shut the doors again," said Hector, who was the first one in, gun drawn, sweeping the room for people.

"Whoever operates this base is going to be alerted that the missile bay doors are opened," said Jim right behind him. Richard pulled Kyle inside behind Christine, and they found themselves on the top level of a very tall metal gantry with an elevator platform to their right. A huge tank-like truck was parked on a small moon rock ledge on the left. It had bouncy-looking wheels and tinted windows. The body was like a box truck but with slanted edges. It was the same color as the lunar soil.

"Let's move Kyle inside that truck and work on him without being seen," said Hector.

"Hurry up and close the doors to the outside," said Richard.

"We're going to run out of oxygen soon," said Jim.

"There have got to be oxygenated rooms below this missile somewhere," said Hector.

"What if it's all missile domes and no habitat?" said Christine.

"We're screwed if that's the case," said Jim.

They rushed Kyle over to the van. The back doors were unlocked. Christine pulled them open and found a sophisticated mobile lab with computers, microscopes, lasers, and small centrifuges. Hector and Richard hoisted Kyle into the truck and laid him down in the middle of the floor. Hector started working on Kyle, while Richard kept guard and Christine's attention was drawn to the equipment.

"The work being done here is very advanced," said Christine.

At the same time, Jim pressed the buttons to close the base doors and then quickly made his way to the truck and joined them.

Hector was already at work on Kyle. He had removed his backpack and pulled out a med bag. He jammed two needles into Kyle's arm and left them there, then connected some tubes to the needles and ran those into another section of his bag. Kyle became much more alert.

"I don't see any signs of internal bleeding, but you're right, you have a couple of broken ribs, left side," said Hector.

Christine glanced at her wrist PDA and read that there was a low level of oxygen inside the vehicle and the level was rising quickly. She unlocked her face mask and slid it up. "The air is oxygenated in here."

They all removed their masks and took in the stale air.

"And the oxygen levels are slowly rising now that the doors are shut," Christine added.

"That means there's people here," said Hector.

"What does this equipment mean to you, Dr. Uy?" said Richard.

"This van is a mobile gravity gradiometer with a helium-3 extractor and subatomic decoupler on board," she said.

"In plain English, please," said Richard.

"It's a sophisticated lab that is used to locate H3 mineral deposits, so they know where to mine. They probably used this lab to locate the spot we're standing on."

"None of that changes the fact that a nuke is in the silo that can be used against the United States," said Hector.

Kyle cleared his throat, looking up at them. "We have to rethink this. We can't use the J5s to blow up this nuclear warhead."

"We have to destroy the nuke up here one way or another. It poses a lethal threat to our national security and world peace," said Richard.

"Look, if I can get inside the controls, I can reconfigure the flight path, and we can send it way out into space, let it explode out there," said Kyle.

"You're kidding right?" said Christine.

Hector finished cleaning up Kyle's wounded arm and zipped his suit back up. Kyle flexed his arm and winced slightly.

"You're not going to feel a thing for the next eight hours," said Hector.

"Do we have any other options?" said Kyle. Having regained full mobility, he removed the J5s from their containers. They were the smallest nuclear bombs ever invented and resembled harmless little cellphones with a small LCD on one side. He handed three to Hector and three to Richard. "You guys take these and plant them around the base while I alter that missile's flight path."

"What's the activation code?" said Hector.

"One, two, three, four," said Kyle.

"You're kidding," said Jim. Hector laughed out loud.

"This is suicide," said Christine.

"For the Chinese," grunted Hector.

THE MINE

THE WAILING ALARM was not loud enough to wake Wen Jun who sat, cross-armed, passed out in front of a wall of monitors displaying the status of every system, door, and machine in the base. He had a difficult time staying awake at the command terminal as was usually the case after a few months of being stationed in Tiāntáng. Something about living here long-term made him overwhelmingly tired. The lack of vitamin D was the biggest culprit. He sometimes required immediate sleep, so he power-napped and shirked his duties until later. The monotony of the routine was having a negative impact on his mental health, but Wen Jun was chosen for this job specifically for his ability to stay focused and work tirelessly in extreme conditions. It was all a sacrifice now for the greater glory he would receive when the world found out about his role in outsmarting America once and for all.

He woke up talking to himself again. "Somebody stop the microwave," he muttered before waking half-asleep, realizing the alarm was really coming from his environmental warning system. The surface gates had been opened briefly and a significant amount of oxygen had been lost.

Wen Jun stood, rubbed his face, and pressed a button that allowed him to toggle through a series of base cameras. One at a time he studied screens to find out who left the base without permission. His gut told him it was Wei Li, who was suffering from Tiāntáng fever worse than anyone else. Wei Li liked to sneak out and go for walks in the crater when he wasn't supposed to. He claimed it helped him not feel so trapped to see the stars and to be away from the confines of the base.

Wen Jun stopped looking at the monitors and walked out of the room and into the central hallway, where Wei Li happened to be walking by. He had his head down and headphones on, oblivious to anything around him. Wei Li was the scrawniest taikonaut, with a bone-thin face but the strength of ten men.

Wen Jun stepped in front of him and stopped him by putting his hand to Wei Li's forehead and pushing gently with one finger. "Why don't you look where you are going?" said Wen Jun.

Wei Li pulled his headphones out and smiled at Wen Jun. "It's only a circle. I can't get lost. How many times do I have to remind you of that?

"Were you out for one of your walks? Out on the surface?" probed Wen Jun.

"No. I'm heading to the gym before I start my shift. I'm operating silo three tonight."

"Have you seen Zhèng Min?" asked Wen Jun while looking down the long carved-out hallway in both directions.

"He's in the galley, eating. I passed him. What's going on?" said Wei Li.

"The missile dome gates were opened for eight minutes a short while ago," said Jun.

"But no one has been up there in days. Do you want me to make sure everything's OK?" said Wei Li.

"Yes. Then report back to me before you head to your shift. There may be a way for you to return home sooner. I'll tell you about it at dinner tonight," said Wen Jun.

This made Wei Li smile. "I'll be right back." He started on his way.

"One more thing," said Wen Jun.

"What?" said Wei Li.

"Put on a breather. The dome has very low oxygen levels," said Wen Jun.

Wei Li nodded and started walking down the stone corridor again. It was bright with lights that lined the ceiling and walls, creating a mesmerizing tube effect. He popped his headphones back in and was a little spaced-out, barely paying attention to where he was going. He kept walking until he came upon a pair of steel doors with the nuclear symbol right in the center of each door. He went over to a set of lockers next to a control box, opened one, pulled out a breather and inspected the tiny oxygen tanks on each side of its three breathing ports to ensure they were full. Satisfied, he slid the breather over his mouth and waved his right arm over a reader that scanned something on the sleeve of his taikonaut-base suit, and the heavy doors started to open slowly.

"Do you hear that? Where's that sound coming from?" said Hector.

They sat quietly and could hear the deep rattling sound of metal doors opening way down below.

"They know we're here," said Christine, nervous and not looking forward to conflict.

"You don't know that. Could be some routine maintenance," said Jim.

"Or work that uses this mobile lab," said Kyle.

"We may have to fight our way out of this," said Hector.

"Don't fire those guns up here next to this missile, OK?" urged Christine.

Hector held out his hand in a calming way.

"Relax. Nobody wants that sucker to blow until we are far away from this place," he said.

"I'm going to slip into the front seat and try to see what's happening out there," said Richard as he climbed through a small pass-through into the front cabin of the mobile lab. It had a soft cushy leather seat, deep and comfortable. He sat in the driver's side, slid down as far as possible, and scanned the area in silence, trying to listen, his nerves on edge.

The high-pitched sound of a small, squeaky lift elevator echoed inside the dome, and they all knew someone was on the way.

"Cargo elevators coming up," whispered Richard.

Hector signaled to Jim to take position on one side of the back door while he got on the other. Using his foot, he demonstrated that he wanted Jim to kick the door as hard as possible when someone tried to open it. Hector nudged the back door and left it slightly ajar to entice someone to check on it. Kyle was sitting on the ground with Christine right behind him, weapons pointed at the door.

Richard watched the small taikonaut lift into frame and appear to be looking down at a handheld device while listening to music. "I see one taikonaut, and he seems distracted," whispered Richard.

Everyone in the back was holding still.

"OK, now he's looking around. He's checking out the control box by the doors we came in. He doesn't look armed at all." Richard slunk down even more, and he peered over the dashboard of the vehicle. "Uh oh. Our boot prints have his attention now. He's looking at where they go. Crap, he's looking right at the truck now. Be ready back there."

Richard unsheathed his moon dagger from its pouch on his right thigh. He gripped it tightly, ready to murder Wei Li if he opened the door. "He's coming this way."

Wei Li stopped walking, pulled his earphones out, and stood still looking at the mobile lab for a moment. He cocked his head, puzzled, then continued walking toward the mobile lab. He followed the boot prints around to the back. The moment he stepped in front of the doors, they swung open with tremendous force, smashing Wei Lei in the face. It all happened so fast.

Wei Li opened his eyes when Hector was in midair, about to land right on him. He rolled clear and got up fast. They traded awkward blows, with Hector smashing him across the jaw with a rounding left hook.

"Americans! Americans!" cried Wei Li before Jim took him down with a football tackle meant to do harm.

Wei Li's voice echoed inside the dome and seemed like an alarm that stayed on for a long few seconds. Hector put him in a tight headlock and ripped off his breather mask, trying to choke him out as fast as possible.

Little Wei Li was much stronger than he appeared and was able to roll them both toward the edge of the platform, struggling for dominance the entire way.

Jim pounced, grabbing Wei Li's feet to stop him from using his legs and pulled the two men back, but Wei Li was able to break free and stand again. He was choking and spitting with his hands up, ready to fight. His eyes were bloodshot, and he was crazed. He could not speak or yell.

Jim and Hector circled Wei Li in silence. Hector saw Richard creeping toward Wei Li, who was backing up.

Jim saw the moon dagger in Richard's right hand. He shook his head no as Richard quickly thrust the blade into Wei Li's back, bringing him to his knees with short gasps of air. Like a trained killer, Richard covered Wei Li's mouth until he passed, visibly disturbed while doing it.

"Was that necessary?" said Jim.

"It was either him or us," said Richard.

"He was going to die anyway," said Hector. "We probably don't have much time before others arrive. Let's rework the plan right here, right now."

"We're going inside the base to place the bombs while Kyle works on the missile. You can stay here with Christine and Kyle if you want, but we have a mission to fulfill," said Richard.

"I'm not sitting up here waiting to die. If you're going down, I'm going too. What about you Christine? You're not trained for this," said Jim.

"Oh yes I am," said Christine, standing outside the van with her moon dagger out. I've been studying martial arts since I could walk. Fighting skills have come in handy more than once walking home in Washington at night."

"Well, all right. We all go. Hiding six small bombs and getting out again should not take us too long unless we meet resistance or are captured," said Hector.

"The faster we are in and out the better," said Jim.

Richard started searching Wei Li's base suit. He pulled

out his iPod and headphones, some crumpled up food wrappers, a pack of gum, and a red plastic card with gold lettering written across the top. "What's this say?"

"This side up," said Christine.

"What, do they have an ATM up here?" joked Hector.

"Maybe it opens doors or locks," said Jim.

"It's all he's carrying," said Richard as he slid the red card into his own pocket and pointed toward the elevator. "Time to move. Are you ready, Kyle?"

"I feel zero pain," said Kyle, standing close to the missile. "I need twenty to thirty minutes. You can set those bombs anywhere. Once armed, we'll have sixty minutes to get the hell out of here."

"What if we end up stuck down below?" said Christine.

"It's been real nice knowing you," said Hector.

"Not funny," said Christine.

"You asked. Now let's roll," said Hector as he led the way across the moon rock ledge and toward the metal gantry. They stepped onto the elevator, and Richard pressed the button. Jim made the sign of the cross as the elevator lowered them into unknown territory.

Christine had a tight grip on the handle of her moon dagger as the elevator descended the side of the gantry. She didn't like any of this and was especially nervous about being tortured if captured. She was well aware of how brutal the Chinese military could be from stories she'd heard from her father who had fled to America right before her birth. To this day, some of her relatives remain trapped in China after the freedom crackdown and social credit system was established. The thought of being physically restricted because someone in the government didn't like you, horrified her entire family and made them lovers of liberty—values that were passed down to Christine. When her father defected to America, he brought his expertise in physics with him and contributed to many top secret military projects. Christine was proud of her family history in the United States and understood that it was now her honor and duty to help defend freedom no matter how difficult it could be.

Hector, Jim, and Richard all had their daggers at the ready. Richard's was slightly bloodstained and menacing-looking, contrasting with his expression of dark shock at what he had done. Jim concluded that his friend had never imagined it would be this bad. But here they were, a group of Americans with small swords in hand, on the moon to take care of business. There were no signs of activity below. Everything seemed normal as the elevator descended.

While the others rode down in the elevator, Kyle carefully made his way across one of the gantry beams that connected to the nose cone of the nuclear missile. He was looking for the brains of the missile's launch computer, so he could reprogram the trajectory and timing. There was always the risk of setting the whole thing off by accident, but he felt no pressing need to let the others know that.

Kyle was confident in Hector's ability to complete the mission on the inside and keep the action clear, so he could do his job here. As he inched his way across, he thought that the best place to send the missile would be as far away from Earth as possible. Since he knew he was already on the far side of the moon, it seemed logical that a perfectly straight flight path would be a safe trajectory away from the sun.

When he reached the end of the gantry, he found a number of small locked panels on the side of the missile about halfway down from his position. Those were the doors he was looking for. Thinking fast, he figured he could harness himself to the gantry using the excess climbing wire and lower himself in between the rafters. He would be a sitting duck if anyone found him, but it was his only option.

He balanced on the beam and attached a clip. He put the matching clip on the other side and threw the leftover wire through one end before the other, creating a loop he could sit in and lower himself with. He eased into position, teetering perilously forward and back until he could maintain balance. He began to lower himself down using his feet to walk down the side of the missile until he reached the right height. He sat straight and began trying to pick open the panel that housed the control board. Sweat beads formed on his forehead despite the cold temperature inside the dome.

Hector was the first to step onto the ground floor when the elevator landed. The massive engine cones from the missile hung thirty feet above their heads, and an eerie silence surrounded them. They stood still outside the elevator, listening for sounds of human activity. Only the occasional tap or ding coming from up above could be heard.

Hector nodded and led the way forward. Jim kept his right flank while Richard and Christine used their eyes to scan every inch of space around them, collecting intel. Giant metal crates lined one side of the silo. On another, fuel tubes protruded out of the wall and hooked up to the lower portion of the rocket. The whole operation was elegantly efficient.

In the center of the room was a human-size double door. Through this was another pass-through airlock, and the door on the other side was open. Hector pointed to the airlock control box and waved Jim over. "Airlock leads somewhere. Keep watch while I check out what's on the other side."

"What are you going to say if you run into someone?" asked Jim.

"Who ordered takeout?" joked Hector.

Jim and Richard chuckled.

"This is not a time for jokes," huffed Christine.

Jim peered through the small window in the airlock to another small window on the other side. Across a hallway was another hollowed-out cave that was lit up. No people could be seen or heard anywhere.

The airlock door hissed when Hector pulled it open and stepped inside. The hallway was clear in both directions, so he waved the rest of them forward. Once inside the base, Hector put his hand on Richard's and Christine's shoulder and pushed them both down into a crouching position. Jim copied the position. They all faced the outer doors.

"Be ready for anything and shoot to kill," said Hector as he stepped into the hallway and took in the inner workings of the base for the first time. The structure was carved right out of the moon rock. The sound of distant machines echoed toward him in an eerie, repetitive whining sound, but there were no other humans. Using hand signals, Hector moved forward first, then waved them up.

Christine marveled at the site of the bored-out hallway the minute she stepped into it. She also gripped her dagger so tightly that it made her hand quiver. Jim and Richard stayed intently focused on their surroundings and took positions on opposite sides to provide cover, pistols in hand.

Hector moved to the end of the short hallway and used

the reflective screen of his wrist PDA to look in both directions down an adjoining hall that crossed theirs. Each side was the same: uneven carved-out corridors with enough room for a truck the size of the mobile lab to drive through. The floors were hardened moon rock that had evidence of frequent foot and vehicle traffic. Hector moved slowly into the open corridor, and when he reached the top, the sloping path led into another cave. High-pitched sounds were emanating from the cave. He looked in all directions, finding no people, no cameras. He waved the rest of them forward again and signaled that he wanted to head straight into the next cave.

They moved quickly and cautiously down the corridor. The whining sounded like a drill and grew louder as they got closer. The corridor rounded slightly to the left and brought them to an uneven blown-out opening that led into a cave awash in blueish light.

A laser drill bore into the moon rock in a far corner of the cave. It was manned by a lone taikonaut who stood on a base with a control system that operated a long mechanical arm. The whole thing was on wheels, and he was moving from left to right and then stopped. The arm extended very high, and the taikonaut directed a red laser beam to dig out a chunk of deep-blue moon rock, which fell into a waiting net below the arm.

"That is a huge rock of pure H3," whispered Christine.

"We have to find cover before he turns around and zaps us with that laser," said Jim.

"Over there," said Hector. He jumped down into the mine and scuttled as fast as possible to the far right, where a pillar of uneven drilled-out moon rock provided a dark corner to hide behind. Jim and Christine crouched right behind him, but Richard jumped down at the exact moment that the taikonaut stopped drilling and suddenly turned around.

The taikonaut's face mask was tinted black, his body strangely perfect and smooth. Richard lay there staring at the taikonaut, wondering if he had been seen. Then the taikonaut's head dropped and his shoulder slumped as if he had suddenly been shut off.

"This is a damn droid," said Richard. He stood up and walked toward it.

"What the hell are you doing?" said Jim.

"He's going to get us all killed, that's what he's doing," said Christine.

Richard stood in front of the taikonaut, which was really a taikobot—an advanced humanoid robot. Up close it was clearly made of machine parts and wires that were housed in a semitransparent plastic body, so it appeared that you were seeing inside someone's body. Richard lifted up the head and let it fall again. He was familiar with the droid because it was identical to one NASA had been developing for many years.

Hector came up beside Richard and pulled him away from the front.

"What if that thing is watching you," said Hector.

Hector sliced its head clean off with one vicious swipe of his moon dagger.

"And that's not going to get us noticed?" asked Richard.

"I've seen enough. We plant the bombs, grab Kyle, and we get the heck out of here," said Hector while pulling out his first J5. He went looking for a place to hide it and came upon some elevated rail tracks that went into a small tunnel along the backside of the cave. He stared into the tunnel using his helmet light, revealing that it was spacious enough to crawl into. "Over here."

Christine and Richard hurried over, but Jim lagged behind inspecting the taikobot and its laser drill before joining the rest of them at the tunnel.

"They mine the H3, then send it through here," Christine replied.

"What would happen to it next?" asked Richard.

"It has to be processed. This tunnel probably leads to some machinery that does the job," she said.

"Do you think they're processing here and shipping it back to Earth?" said Jim.

"It appears that way. I'll know more if we find the machine itself," said Christine.

"We should follow this tunnel," said Richard.

"Agreed. Inside there is going to be a perfect spot to plant a bomb," said Hector.

"I'll go first," said Richard as he jumped up and grabbed the ledge and pulled himself onto the track platform. He put out a hand and helped Hector up. Jim climbed up on his own and assisted Christine.

Hector turned on his helmet light and dimmed it to provide enough light to illuminate two feet in front of their position. The tunnel was lined with electrical wiring at the top that hung loosely but not low enough to touch them. Soon they were deep inside and no longer visible from the outside.

Wen Jun stood over Wei Li's dead body beside the lunar surface vehicle next to the missile. He was flanked by his second in command, Li Jing. They almost didn't believe what they were seeing. Wang Xi came running toward them.

"What happened to him?" said Wang Xi before he was close enough to realize that Wei Li was dead and bloody around the middle.

"Murdered, stabbed in the back by somebody," said Wen Jun as he rolled him over to expose the bloody dagger gash.

"How is this possible?" said Wang Xi.

Wen Jun pointed around his own feet, to all the boot prints and evidence of a struggle.

"We have visitors. More than one," said Wen Jun.

"I ran through the central hall and didn't see anyone," said Wang Xi.

"This door was breached fifteen minutes ago," said Li Jing. He clicked a stun gun on, and it buzzed with current.

"We must find whoever did this and apprehend them before they sabotage our operation," ordered Wen Jun.

"No doubt that is what they're here to do," said Li Jing.

"Not on my watch," said Wen Jun.

"Do you want me to notify Beijing command and control?" asked Wang Xi.

"No. I must handle it alone," said Wen Jun.

"Hostiles inside Tiāntáng is reason to notify them, Commander. President Xian needs to know if we've been discovered," urged Wang Xi.

"The missile is secure and that is what matters," said Wen Jun as he raised his hand up to his mouth. They all spied around in silence for signs that the intruders were still nearby. Using hand signals, Wen Jun motioned for them to split up and search the entire base.

At the same time, Kyle was dripping with sweat, and his fingers were turning blue. He had successfully shimmied himself under the area where the taikonauts were standing and where the gantry structure connected to the moon rock. He hid under a perfect-size beam and was hanging on for dear life. His injured arm trembled. He heard the taikonauts shuffling about above him. The crackle of their stun guns coming to life, doors opening and closing on the van. He saw one of them run to the elevator and ride it back down in a fighting stance with the gun activated. That's when a pair of taikonaut boots landed on the metal gantry beam he was hiding under and started to walk across it toward the missile, where he had left the panel door wide open with wires hanging out.

"Someone's tampered with the missile," warned Wang Xi.

Kyle sweat as Wang Xi's boots turned around and stood still facing where he was hiding. Kyle used shallow breathing to keep as quiet as possible. The boots took two steps toward Kyle and stomped on both fingertips.

Kyle dropped his hand and was able to keep his ankles wrapped tightly against the beam, holding himself upside down like a bat, then he fell.

"I want him alive!" yelled Wen Jun.

Wang Xi ran across the beam and hopped up onto the ledge, running toward the elevator beside Wen Jun.

When Kyle hit the ground with a breath-stealing thud, he was immediately met face-to-face with Li Jing's stun gun. Kyle gasped for air as Li Jing pointed the stun gun directly at him and pulled the trigger. Kyle blacked out while his falling scream and thud were still echoing through the base, into the mine, and deep inside the tunnels.

"What was that horrible sound?" asked Christine.

"That sounded like Kyle," said Jim from the back.

"I'm going to go look. Just keep moving. I will catch up," said Jim as he shimmied around and started back toward the opening.

"Be careful," said Christine.

Soon Jim could see into the mine cave and nobody was inside it. The destroyed taikobot still lay on the ground untouched. Jim slid down into the mine and ran back to the entrance. Peering around the corner he spied two tai-konauts kneeling over Kyle's body underneath the missile. They were binding his hands and feet; he presumed Kyle was still alive.

That's when Li Jing crossed directly into Jim's line of sight but didn't notice him standing there. Jim recoiled against the wall as Li Jing prowled the hallway. He had a stun gun in his right hand.

Jim used his wrist PDA to peek back down the hall as Li Jing walked away from him, heading in another direction. The other two taikonauts started pulling Kyle's lifeless body down the hall in a different direction. When the coast was clear, Jim leaped down into the mine and scurried back to his crew inside the tunnel.

Jim pulled himself up into the tunnel and started crawl-ing as fast as he could toward them. The space became increasingly cramped the farther he went, with a little room on both sides and barely enough height for Jim to rest on his knees. Rail tracks on top of bumpy moon rock was not fun to traverse, but light at the end of the tunnel meant they were not trapped.

"What happened?" whispered Christine, who was at the end of the line.

"They got Kyle, and now they're looking for us. As far as I can tell they're armed with stun guns," said Jim.

"They were not expecting visitors," said Richard.

"Our cover has been blown and the bomb clock is now ticking," said Jim.

"We don't have any options other than to press forward through to the end and fight our way out if it comes to that," said Hector.

Hector fished around in his side pocket and pulled out one of the micro nukes. "We're going to execute the plan as fast as possible," Hector said as he punched in the code and activated the micro nuke before sliding it into a cut-out section of the wall by his head. He pushed it deep inside and left it there. "Based on what this place looked like on the surface, I'm betting the mines connect via these tunnels. All we have to do is leave bombs planted in each one and then disappear before anyone catches up to us."

"Easier said than done," said Jim.

"What about Kyle?" said Christine.

"We ain't leaving without him. I've fought bigger armies in tighter conditions on Earth," said Hector.

"The last place we want to be caught is in here," urged Richard as he nudged Hector to start crawling again. When Christine passed the area where the bomb was laid, she paused and lingered on it before continuing.

Li Jing had already taken up position inside the mine that the Americans were heading toward. He hid inside a small control room at the bottom of the exhaust silo in the middle of the mine that housed master controls for the taikobots. He waited at a computer terminal and kept his eyes on the tunnel.

The first bit of blue helmet poked out of the tunnel and looked both ways. Li Jing rapidly input commands into the touch screen, heart racing, when another American came out of the tunnel and stood in silence beside the first one.

Sitting ducks.

Li Jing pressed a few more commands and took control over two taikobots. They came online and swerved their laser drill machines toward the Americans, blinding them with intense white light from the tip of the laser gun.

"Get down!" yelled Hector, pulling his moon dagger from its leg sheath and running toward the droid nearest him. Richard dove in the other direction as a beam of red light obliterated a chunk of moon rock right above their heads.

Inside the tunnel, Jim shielded Christine with his body while moon rock rained down on them.

Hector charged the taikobot again, swinging to decapitate it as he did to the last one. The laser shot out, and he miraculously intercepted the beam with the dagger blade, which lit up like a fire sword and shot the beam right back at the droid, making it explode into bits. Hector was stunned and saw Richard circling away from the other droid in an awkward sidestep to escape getting zapped.

"I need backup in mine number six. I'm in the control room and found two Americans in here—hurry bring a lethal weapon," Li Jing said as the door was kicked in by

Hector, who rushed him into the corner and held the burning hot moon dagger to his neck.

"Shut down the lasers!" demanded Hector. Li Jing froze. Hector jammed his elbow into Li Jing's chest while he stabbed the control panel until the computer system blanked out. Outside of the control room, the remaining droid's laser started going berserk, firing in multiple directions and creating a heavy fog of moondust that started filling the mine. Richard was on the floor crawling to safety when the laser swiped over his right foot, leaving a burning line across his Achilles. He screamed, falling to the ground and writhing in severe pain.

Hector and Li Jing burst out of the silo room, fighting over the dagger. Li Jing slipped away when Hector spun around and decapitated the droid while its laser burned inches from his face. He jumped onto the machine itself and went to sever the laser gun when an explosion and a bright flash of light threw both of their bodies into the wall with violent force. Kaboom! Another huge blast of pressure crushed them when a small missile slammed into the floor, leaving a gaping hole where they once stood.

Standing in the mine entrance with the bazooka, Zhèng Min waited while the weapon warmed up for its next shot, making a deep whirring sound that echoed inside the cave.

"You will not succeed!" shouted Zhèng Min.

Hector was able to pull himself to cover behind the central silo. Richard tried crawling toward him, but he was disoriented and confused. Hector pulled his pistol, rolled out and started blasting toward Zhèng Min in the entrance of the mine. The fog was so thick now it became impossible for them to keep eyes on each other for more than a moment.

When Hector missed Zhèng Min, each bullet blasted an oversize hole in the moon rock that it hit. Zhèng Min pulled the trigger and another missile landed nearby and threw Hector's body against the wall, crumpling him like a rag doll. A hail of bullets followed, drilling Hector in the chest over and over, killing him instantly but missing Richard.

The fog dust was at its thickest when Richard was hit by a jolting stun gun that stopped him cold. He crawled around lost when Zhèng Min smashed him in the face with his boot heel while again pulling the trigger on the stun gun until Richard blacked out.

"I caught one of them alive, and I killed one inside mine five. I'm bringing the alive one to the control room," said Zhèng Min as he pulled Richard's limp body by the helmet, disappearing into the fog while Jim and Christine watched from the safety of the tunnel. They were lucky, Zhèng Min never thought to look inside.

"It's only a matter of time before we're found too," said Christine.

"We ran out of options the minute we stepped foot in this base, but I cannot leave these guys behind, turn tail, and let them die up here," said Jim.

"I'm not suggesting that. I'm willing to fight and try and save them, but at some point, we all run out of time."

"You keep moving while I go retrieve the J5s inside Hector's pockets. We can probably buy our way out of here by threatening to blow the place up."

"What about the already activated bomb?" said Christine.

"They detonate in approximately forty-five minutes," said Jim.

"We could fake a surrender and hold them hostage with the remaining bombs," she said.

"I got a better idea. We'll arm and place as many as possible and if we're caught we do your idea," said Jim.

"But there's nowhere to hide," said Christine.

"That's why we have to keep going forward, keep planting bombs and look for the exit and our crew," said Jim.

"That taikonaut said he was bringing Richard to some control room. We have to locate where that is," said Christine.

Jim retrieved the remaining J5s and they crawled out of the tunnel and ran to the next one across the elevated tracks. Once inside the next tunnel, Jim took bomb number two, activated it, waited for six short blinks of red light before the countdown clock initiated. He handed it to Christine.

"What do you want me to do with this?" she said.

"Put it under the track behind your feet, right up against the rail," he said.

Christine, hands shaking, placed the activated J5 under the rail. They started crawling in the direction of the next exit at the end of the tunnel.

Blood from Richard's smashed nose spattered across the wall as Wen Jun busted him again with a heavy flashlight. The base lights were flickering now. Power was going in and out.

"I said, how many are you!"

"Only… me," said Richard. His helmet was cracked in half and partially dangling from the back. The visor was a ridge of broken glass in front of his bloodied face. His hands were bound together behind him.

Wen Jun walked over to a cabinet door and opened it. Kyle's dead body tumbled to the ground. He laughed as Richard's breathing increased and his eyes watered. "Was this man a friend of yours, or did he arrive on his own spaceship?"

Richard said nothing.

Wen Jun wailed on him again with the flashlight, cracking his skull above his left eye.

"He came in his own ship," mumbled Richard.

Wen Jun leaned in, thinking he had finally broken through.

"What did you say?"

"He came in his own ship, and so did I. We're in a private spaceship club. We wanted to get to the moon and back," chuckled Richard, delirious and out of his mind.

"What are you telling me, American pig?" said Wen Jun.

"I'm telling you… we came on a private spaceship from Texas, and when we found your illegal base, we decided it was high time to kick your commie ass right the hell out," said Richard with a sudden burst of clarity.

Wen Jun took Richard's moon dagger, flipped it around, and ran it right through the toes of his left boot and into the floor, making Richard yell out from the bottom of his gut. "Don't play games with me, black devil."

Richard's shoulders slumped down. He seemed defeated, spitting blood, struggling to breathe again. Broken.

"It's three of us. We came in one small ship."

"Who told you to come here? Uncle Sam?" said Wen Jun.

"Ya see… that's the funny part," mused a crazed-looking Richard, who had been secretly working his hands free the entire time. Little by little he was getting there. He swayed forward and back as if about to pass out. "We really did come here all on our own from a free country where a guy can build a spaceship if he wants to," sputtered Richard.

"And you think you can take the moon from China?" Wen Jun chuckled.

"It was never yours to begin with," sputtered Richard.

"We beat you at your own game. The moon is ours now," said Wen Jun.

"Consider the claim denied, you son of a bitch!" Richard pulled the moon dagger out of his foot and sliced right up the middle of Wen Jun's body with the tip, cutting through his suit and leaving a bloody gash across his chest. Richard stumbled up from the chair, unbalanced, and lunged at Wen Jun, who leaped into the air and kicked him in the teeth while grabbing the falling dagger by its handle in midair. He mercilessly plunged the dagger into the back of Richard's neck and pulled the blade out.

"That's for killing Wei Li." Wen Jun stabbed the moon rock wall beside him, and the knife went in easily. His eyes lit up. He pulled the dagger out, slid it under his belt, then went to the lockers. He kicked Kyle's body out of the way and opened a second locker using a code. The door popped opened, and Wen Jun had his pick of weapons. He pocketed two handguns and lay a rifle across his shoulder. He had to take care of this breach quickly. If things got too hot, he would be left for dead. Knowing this, Wen Jun ran to the doorway and down into the corridor, where the lights flickered. Once he found and killed every one of the Americans, it would be another notch on his belt as China's long-awaited modern-day war hero. "Li Jing, do you read me," whispered Wen Jun, peering down the corner through the scope of his rifle.

"I'm in mine three surveying the damage with Zhèng Min."

"We've killed three Americans. Are there more?" said Wen Jun as he made his way toward mine three, ready to be ambushed.

"It doesn't look that way. I doubt anyone could build a spaceship capable of transporting more than three people in America these days," chuckled Li Jing.

"Somebody is going to be missing them," said Zhèng Min.

"You two finish sweeping the base while I check and stabilize the power. Meet me in the command room when you're done. If you come across any more Americans, kill them," said Wen Jun.

"It will be my pleasure," said Zhèng Min.

"What are we going to do with their bodies?" said Li Jing.

"We should make scarecrows out of them and place them in the basin to warn others," joked Zhèng Min.

LONE SURVIVORS

JIM HAD HIS pistol pointed directly toward the entrance to the mine Li Jing and Zhèng Min were currently standing in. Li Jing was looking into the tunnel with a flashlight, while Zhèng Min inspected the silo in the middle.

Sweat dripped down Jim's nose as he watched. The struggle to keep his emotions in check after overhearing about the murder of Kyle, Hector, and Richard was compounded by the fact he and Christine would be next. Christine kept her gaze and pistol pointed in the opposite direction.

"Looks like they went through here, but we found them on the other side," said Li Jing.

"We need to locate the ship they arrived on. It can't be too far," said Zhèng Min.

"Do you think they were military or mercenaries?" said Li Jing.

"Americans are always both, and that means things are going to worsen now. We have to prepare for more invaders," said Zhèng Min.

"Bring this corpse to the command room and search it. I'll continue to sweep the area and help Wen Jun with the generator," said Li Jing as he walked out of the mine and turned left.

Zhèng Min grabbed Hector's body by the neck area and dragged it to a cart. He threw it on, then pushed the cart to the service elevator and rode it up. At the top, he stepped out of the mine and took a right.

After minutes of silence, Jim touched Christine on the shoulder. She wiped tears from her eyes and looked back at him to find distress in his eyes too. "I think they're gone now. If we just keep moving in the opposite direction of them, we'll find our way out. Before we move on… ," he said while activating another bomb right there. He placed it under the tracks they were on. "Two down, four to go."

"We're leaving as soon as we find the exit, no matter how many bombs are left," said Christine.

"Damn right. I'll activate and leave them in the middle of the room if I have to. Our goal now is to beat them to finding our ship. If you remember what this place looked like on the surface it's one big circle. Eventually, we are going to be right back where we started," said Jim.

"Why don't we backtrack from here and escape the way we came," pleaded Christine.

"Because they'll kill us on sight and we're outnumbered," said Jim.

"Understood."

"We're in a hot zone now. We've lost three of our men. Be ready to fire your weapon at all times because it's either us or them," Jim said as they crawled toward the next mine, stopping from time to time to listen. After a few minutes, they reached the exit and climbed down from the tracks. This mine was the biggest so far and had huge missing pockmarks where moon rock had been excavated. Christine stopped and picked up a small light-blue pebble from the ground. She brought it up close to her face and it was translucent. She slipped the stone into a small pocket on the back of her glove. Jim kept sweeping the mine with his eyes, looking for any sign of movement. Suddenly bright light from above lit up the whole place. Christine and Jim scurried to the next tunnel like mice caught in the night.

The contents from Kyle's, Hector's, and Richard's spacesuits were spread out on the floor in the command room. The climbing gear told them the ship is not in the Von Kármán. The weapons told them they came looking for trouble. One thing was missing— identification of any kind. This was the biggest clue in determining it was, in fact, a hostile military operation that had failed.

"Everyone is named Smith. This is CIA deception for sure," said Wen Jun as the power was restored and full lights came on. The base monitoring cameras slowly popped back on one by one. Wen Jun watched them. He studied each and every mine and there was no movement. He checked the missile silo, and all was quiet there too.

Li Jing returned and flanked Wen Jun as he started to review the base's system status.

"We need to notify… ," said Li Jing.

"First find their ship. We must have every detail in order before I tell Xian anything," said Wen Jun.

"But you're going against emergency protocol," said Li Jing.

Wen Jun faced him. "We are the keepers of the doomsday bomb. Unless you want to be imprisoned back home for failing to hold this sacred ground, I think you should follow my lead."

"Why will we be held accountable for being attacked?" asked Li Jing.

"Because we didn't see them coming," said Wen Jun.

"You mean you didn't, Commander. You're the one who sits in here all day doing nothing but watching screens," said Li Jing.

"Are you questioning my leadership?" said Wen Jun.

"No. I'm overriding you. Step aside," insisted Li Jing as he pushed Wen Jun out of the way and pressed the buttons to initiate an emergency call directly to Beijing. Wen Jun pushed back, but Li Jing easily overpowered him and got him into a headlock.

Jim placed the third bomb in a dark crevice of moon rock, and he and Christine moved through the tunnel. Christine stopped and looked up. There was a closed hatch. She turned her head back at Jim and pointed up. He got under it, too, and studied the hatch in silence. It had a metal wheel handle and was exactly like the door to a submarine.

"You want out of here?" asked Jim.

"Maybe this connects to the way out?" said Christine, lowering her pistol to her side.

"Let's find out," Jim said as he set down the pistol, positioned himself under the hatch and started to crank it open. The metal wheel squeaked with each turn, so he went extra slow. Jim stopped twisting and listened. He cocked his head trying to listen more intently. No sounds were a welcome relief. He turned the wheel three more times and the hatch fell open. Jim stared up at a steel ladder built into a wall. About twenty steps in all. They led somewhere he couldn't see from his vantage point.

"Anything?" asked Christine.

"Looks like it could be some kind of an emergency exit," said Jim. He pulled himself up and started to climb the metal ladder, drawing his gun halfway to the top, and found himself in a pitch-black space. He flipped on his helmet light. Thick cables in shiny black wrapping hung on the walls and ceiling of the narrow hallway at the top. He knew where he was immediately.

"What is it?" asked Christine from the bottom of the ladder.

"Power and data cables run through here. They will probably lead us to the power room and maybe the missile silo," he said.

"Let's go for it."

"We could end up stuck."

"We're already stuck," she said.

Jim climbed up into the narrow hallway while Christine started to climb up behind him, happy to be out of the tunnel below.

"Close the hatch so we leave no trace if they look in the tunnels again," said Jim.

Christine climbed down the ladder a few rungs, reached down and pulled up the hatch. It was much heavier than it appeared to be, and she had to use all of her strength to heave it into place. The sound of the metal hatch slamming shut echoed loudly. She froze, staring up at Jim with apologetic eyes.

Jim nodded and used his hands to spin a circle in the air. His way of silently telling her to seal the hatch.

After a few slow cranks, she climbed up the rest of the way and joined him up in the passageway that stretched away from the ladder about thirty yards.

"I see another hatch," said Jim.

"We took a shortcut over the middle," said Christine.

Jim crawled to it, grabbed the wheel, and turned it slow and quiet, looking back at Christine. "Be ready to cover me."

She pulled her pistol out, raised it, and aimed it at the hatch door on the floor in front of her.

Two more full rotations and the hatch door fell open. Bright light filled the corridor, Jim leaned back and pulled his pistol too. They both slid forward and peeked down into the well-lit room filled with cables and wires connecting to giant computers and generators.

"Jackpot. We found the brains of this place," said Jim.

"We've already crossed three silos and might be right back at the missile silo. How much time do we have left?" Christine said.

"Thirty minutes. We go down in, cut the power again, and slip out in darkness," said Jim.

"If we cut the power, the elevator won't work," said Christine.

"Can you climb up the gantry?" he said.

"I'll climb up whatever I have to get out of here alive," she said.

Jim smiled at her. "They killed our friends but we're going to finish the job."

Jim shimmied over the hatch and climbed down the ladder to the ground about six feet below, pointing his weapon in all directions along the way. Christine climbed down and stood beside him in the same ready-to-shoot pose.

"Seems empty," said Jim as they found themselves in a long and deep room.

Mainframe computer terminals lined one side, while a floor to ceiling multipart generator and air purification system was embedded into another wall. Thick cables connected the two areas and also went up into the ceiling where they diverged at multiple points.

"They dug this base out like termites," said Jim.

"Termites aren't this efficient," said Christine.

"How do we shut it all down?" said Jim.

Christine moved toward the computers and started to look through the systems. Jim found the only door and stood guard by it while she searched.

"This is unexpected," said Christine.

"What does it say?" asked Jim.

"According to the computer log, this system was first turned on and ran its first program back in the year 2008," she said.

"A moon base has been here for sixteen years?" said Jim.

"And they have been successfully processing H3 for the past two. Come here. I found a schematic of the entire base. We are right down the hall from a science lab and the missile bay," she said.

Jim walked to Christine and looked over her shoulder. "Just show me where the exit is. The whole place is going to blow in like twenty minutes. We should run."

"Wait. I need to find my way inside the lab. You don't understand the significance. Processed H3 means China is producing fusion energy," she said.

"I do understand. That's why they have a doomsday bomb protecting this base. And if the death missile is not destroyed up here, we're going to spark World War III down there. I have three bombs left, and one is going right… here," Jim said while activating it, then sliding it behind the computer terminal.

"What are you going to do with the last two?" Christine said.

Jim took them out, activated both and placed them at opposite ends of the room. "Put your visor up and turn on your oxygen system. I'm cutting the power and the air in here."

Christine followed his instructions, and as soon as her air system started to flow, she felt more alert and energized.

Jim did the same, then went to the farthest set of wires on the wall. It was clearly the central connection bank, where all the systems meet. The moon dagger sliced right through the cables. Red hazard siren lights activated with an alarm. "Light's out," said Jim as he pulled Christine toward the exit door and signaled for her to stand back while he opened it. She took up a position out of sight with her weapon pointed at the door. Jim glanced back and nodded. She nodded back. He opened the door, ready to kill whatever may be waiting on the other side.

Wen Jun and Li Jing had to set their differences aside when the alarms started to wail. They armed themselves with every weapon available. Li Jing loaded shells into a sawed-off shotgun and cocked it.

"I told you there were more!" said Zhèng Min as he connected a small metal box to his gun, which converted it into a flamethrower.

"There could be more than one ship that landed," said Li Jing.

"This is an invasion," said Zhèng Min.

"Search every single room, tunnel, and crevice. Shoot to kill. After we secure Tiāntáng, we head to the surface," said Wen Jun.

"I got the tunnels," said Zhèng Min.

"Come with me to the lab," said Wen Jun to Li Jing.

"Let's hit them from both directions at the same time, flush them out," said Zhèng Min as the three of them ran out of the room in a tight formation, then split up.

Zhèng Min ran toward the mine. Li Jing and Wen Jun ran in the opposite direction toward the lab and power room. It didn't matter if the Americans had figured out the base was circles of connected underground tunnels because the taikonauts were certain they would run into them and have a chance at stopping the takeover in progress.

Zhèng Min hopped down into the mine ready to shoot. He rushed toward the tunnels with multiple boot prints on the ground around the entrance. "I'm standing outside the transport tunnel in mine three. They were here and went through the mine tunnels. I'm burning through every one," he said while clicking the switch and igniting his flamethrower. A blue pilot light danced in the muzzle of the weapon.

After climbing up and crouching down, he moved forward one track at a time, inching his way along, stopping to listen for a moment before moving some more. Inspecting every inch of track, he neared the area where the first bomb had been planted into the wall. He caught a faint white light coming from the tiny cut out section. He cocked his head, reached in with his hand, grabbed it, and pulled out a sophisticated micro nuke with a countdown clock showing only fifteen minutes remaining.

"Uh, Commander Wen Jun. We're in trouble," said Zhèng Min.

Jim poked his head out of the door and saw another carved-out corridor. They were on the north side of the lunar base, but he couldn't tell the difference between this corridor and the one they had first entered. The same red lights flashed in the halls. Distant sounds of people running echoed down the corridor toward them. After looking both ways, he pulled Christine and bolted to his left until they came to the doors to the processing lab. Jim kicked them in, and they rushed inside, guns drawn, and found themselves in a room packed with sophisticated science equipment set up around an older-looking central machine in the middle of the lab.

Christine turned on her helmet light, went to the machine in the middle, and circled it, wide-eyed. It was the size of a small fridge, had clear tubes feeding blueish liquid into one side and a tray door on the other. The machine was still operational on some kind of backup battery. She marveled at it, wondering what was going on inside.

"They know we're in here," barked Jim.

Christine pulled on the tray door and revealed three translucent poker-chip-size disks set in molded black cases. "Sweet lord, they did it. These disks. They're pure helium-3 in crystalline form. One chip this size… is power for hundreds of years."

"Take them and let's go," urged Jim.

"I… I can't believe this. Come here," said Christine.

"Hurry up and grab them all. We're running out of alive time!"

"Jim, you have to see this with your own eyes to believe it."

Jim ran over and stood beside her, looking down to where she was pointing. A metal tag on the machine read *US Department of Energy*.

"The fusion machine is American made?" said Jim.

"That is an official DOE tag," she said.

"What the hell?"

"Perhaps you weren't told everything about the mission like I wasn't," she said.

"Government lies, people die," said Jim.

"How long ago was this machine invented? How many wars over oil and resources could have been avoided if this was put to use a long time ago?" said Christine.

Pop-pop-pop!

Before Jim could answer, a bullet smashed into his shin, sending him to the ground screaming. Christine dove on top of him, but Jim threw her off and returned fire in the direction of the door.

Wen Jun unloaded his weapon at Jim and Christine but missed as they rolled behind a row of equipment he would not shoot at.

"Come out with your hands up, you dirty Americans," shouted Wen Jun.

Jim and Christine glanced at each other and knew what had to be done.

"Aim for the face," asked Jim.

"Got it," said Christine.

"Go," said Jim as a firefight broke out when he and Christine rolled in opposite directions while blasting Wen

Jun and Li Jing with a hailstorm of bullets at the same time. Li Jing and Wen Jun didn't expect the aggression.

Pop, pop, pop—Christine's gun kept Li Jing on the defense long enough for her to move closer to him. Pop, pop, pop, pop, pop—Jim's weapon kept Wen Jun dodging away. Jim and Christine overwhelmed them.

When Jim was close enough, he ran around the hardware Wen Jun was ducking behind, kicked him in the jaw, then drew his moon dagger and chopped off Wen Jun's left hand with a downward slice.

Christine shot Li Jing square in the kneecap on her way to the door, ruining any chance he had for quick retaliation. He flailed in pain, attempting to shoot back, but his gun was blasted out of his hand by a missed shot from Jim, who had fired from the other side of the room.

"Run and start climbing! I'll catch up!" ordered Jim.

"You almost killed me!" she yelled back.

"You're still here!" he screamed.

Christine ran out through the same door they had come in, with the pistol in her right hand and the H3 samples tucked into her chest pocket. All she had to do was make it back to the missile silo without getting killed.

Her heart thumped inside her chest. The adrenaline rush of being in a gunfight was visceral and manic. Survival mode kicked in, and she sprinted like an animal who was determined to make it out of the chase alive.

THE ESCAPE

WEN JUN ROLLED Jim's legs out from under him. Jim fell forward, went to roll back toward Wen Jun and shoot but was met with a wheel kick, dislocating his shoulder, sending him reeling. He landed, rolled, and searched for his pistol when it felt like a truck landed on his back. He was pinned under a heavy piece of equipment that had been pushed on top of him. A surge of panicked adrenaline supercharged him. He shimmied out, turned on Wen Jun with his dagger, and jammed it into the bottom of his boot, going straight through and sticking out the other end.

Wen Jun wailed in pain, found Jim's pistol on the floor, and grabbed it when Zhèng Min burst into the room, catching him by surprise.

"They planted bombs on timers in the base—we have less than fifteen minutes to get out of here, Commander!" said Zhèng Min.

Wen Jun watched Jim crawling away. He pointed the pistol at Jim while backing out of the room with Zhèng Min.

"I don't have to kill you. You can stay here and burn for your patriotism," said Wen Jun. Once they were in the hall, they closed and sealed the door from the outside.

"Well, damn," sighed Jim, slouched in the corner of the mangled lab, his entire body aflame with pain, blood dripping from his lower lip. Sparks popped from broken wires. Smashed glass was everywhere, including bits from his destroyed face mask. The technology and science around him would soon be long gone from humanity. Jim had been in a lot of bad situations before, but this one topped them all. Trapped alone in a room in an underground moon base that was about to be blown off the lunar surface seemed like an ironic way to die in his mind. It made him chuckle at the unthinkable way he was going to perish. Jim was an inventor who loved space. Born a free man in a free country, he built a ship and made the mistake of giving his government a ride into battle. There was no winner, and what would come to pass on Earth next was going to be really bad. Maybe the end of it all.

He pulled his sore body up and rushed toward the back of the room where he had entered from the ceiling with Christine. He pushed on the door and it wouldn't budge. He was worried about Christine more than anything else. She was going to die up here too, and it was because of his lousy planning. He started throwing things at the door. Chairs, computers, lab equipment. Rage gave him a new source of strength.

Christine was hiding under the exhaust cone of the nuke as Zhèng Min and Wen Jun climbed their way up the gantry to escape. No sign of Jim made her heart sink. She had to find out if he was still alive. The horror of dying alone up here made her cry as she dashed back into the base in search of Jim. She ran through the corridor until she came to the blocked doors to the lab.

A heavy machine was in front of the door; she tried

to move it. She heaved and pushed so hard that her eyes felt like they might pop out of her head. She got it to slide enough for the door to open slightly.

"Jim! I'm here!" she cried. "Jim! Are you in there? Can you hear me? I don't want to die alone," she cried.

"I hear you."

Jim's bloodied hand poked through the door and grasped it. The door started pushing out, Jim grunting the whole time. Tears rolled down Christine's cheeks as they pried the door open enough for him to fall out. He was a bloody mess but still in one piece.

They embraced each other. The lights still flashing, a weird vapor started to trickle around the base. Christine's oxygen light blinked. She ran out as they started back through the base toward the missile silo. She flipped her visor up as the fog was thickening fast and hovering around their knees. The stench made them both gag.

"I know rocket fuel when I smell it. That's the nuke warming up," said Jim as they rounded the corridor and ran through the open-airlock doors. Running out of oxygen was a guarantee.

"I remember seeing suits in the mobile lab we hid in," said Christine.

"We gotta climb to live," said Jim, as they moved to the gantry ladder and started up the hundreds of steps that felt like it took forever. When they reached the top, lightheadedness hit Christine hard. Jim knew the oxygen level was dangerously low and started to slow his breathing to think.

They were disoriented and confused. The mobile lab was gone, taken by Wen Jun and Zhèng Min, who had escaped and left the doors open.

Jim spotted Wei Li's body lying on the floor. He still had a breather on—the light face mask with a limited amount of oxygen. Jim remembered seeing a whole locker of them below. "I'll be right back," he said to Christine.

Jim skipped the stairs and scaled down the side of the gantry. It was impossible to see at the bottom. He gagged and spit. His eyes were watering nonstop. The heat from the rocket made his skin feel like it was on fire.

He touched ground, ran in the general direction of the lockers and felt around until he found them. He opened one and found the breathers—four of them—he pulled one down over his own face and puked right into it. He pulled the mask off and wiped it, put it back on and took deep breaths, starting to have a clear head again while running back to the gantry.

At the top, he found Christine on the floor passed out but still breathing. Jim slid her helmet off, put a breather on her and started pumping her chest. She gagged and woke up, sucking in the air. Her eyes darted up with surprise. Jim tilted his head up. The dome latches were coming undone and the dome was starting to unfold.

Jim lifted Christine, flung her over his shoulders, and made for the gate. He ran-hopped through it and kept going. The amount of oxygen they now had was barely enough to last them back to the ship.

Ice crystals began to form on Christine's forehead and hair. Without the proper protection of a helmet they both were getting burned by the extreme cold temperatures. Jim shook his head at the top of the base entrance and powered through the freezing pain. A bright pop of light made him fall forward and let go of Christine. She went flying, landing on her side. Jim leaped over to her and also landed sideways. That's when they spotted an escape ship taking off from the far side of the base, blasting off the lunar surface and burning fuel brightly as it ascended.

Jim helped Christine up, and they clumsily raced toward the crater wall a half mile away. Behind them, the nuke smoked up in the silo like a simmering volcano. Jim didn't know how much time was left, just the steps needed to make it back to safety. He kept going like a machine designed to perform its function. He fell to the ground and grabbed at his head, breaking off chunks of forehead ice and rubbing his face to try and warm it a little. Christine helped him up. Her own head covered in a blanket of ice crystals.

They made it to the crater wall together and found their climbing gear right where it had been left. Christine was the only one with a functioning pulley belt, so they held each other and connected the wire rope through the loops. Everything happened in slow motion due to the extreme cold. She pressed the button. The line grew taut and started pulling them up, both freezing and holding on to each other for dear life. Jim's head was buried in her bosom like a child to his mother.

The winch wound them up in slow steady moves. As they neared the top, the missile blasted out of the silo.

"God...help us," said Christine as they witnessed the first nuclear missile on the moon lift off. As far as they knew, World War III had already started.

At the top, Christine helped Jim over the ledge, and they leaned on each other all the way back to the ship. Jim pulled her up the ramp and into the airlock with him. They were both shivering violently as Jim worked the airlock door to open the ship.

"My hands, they're f-f-f-frozen," Jim said.

Christine used her deadened hands to push down on the latch with him. The breathers were running out of oxygen, their faces were covered in extreme frostbite, and their hands were useless, but somehow the latch popped, the door opened, and they fell inside and onto the cabin floor, shivering to the point of hardly being able to function.

The door closed behind them, and Jim used his foot to kick on a master button, sealing the airlock and starting up the ship's reserve power. Lights came on, and oxygen started to whirl around the cabin.

"Oh, t-t-t-thank God," said Christine.

"Look up," said Jim as he gazed out through the viewport at the moving light of the nuclear missile's engine cone as it was likely heading for Earth. They stood up and moved right up close to the viewport and looked out together.

"The nuke is going to pass the escape pod," said Jim.

"Where on Earth is it going to hit?" said Christine, shaken and terrified for their home.

"Most likely targets are New York City or Los Angeles," said Jim as he pulled her close. They were like a framed picture of man and woman watching the beginning of the end of the human race together. Christine put her head on Jim's chest and a tear rolled down her cheek when suddenly the whole cabin filled with blinding white light. The missile detonated roughly five thousand miles out. The explosion shot a vibrant spectacle of light and fire in every direction at once. Jim held Christine as strong winds from the missile's wake blew past them and rocked the ship.

The taikonaut escape pod was obliterated by the nuclear detonation as radioactive energy rippled out in all directions. All that remained was an eerie glowing mass that made it seem like Earth had a second sun for a moment. Jim and Christine cried.

"Kyle got the job done," said Jim.

"Mission complete, I guess," said Christine, wiping her face.

They were both dirty, bloody, exhausted, and probably doomed to die of cancer after the blast of radiation washed over them.

"What are we going to do now?" asked Christine.

"We're going home," said Jim.

"Do you think the escape pod made it?" she said.

"I doubt it. It had to have been overtaken by the blast," he said.

"If you're right, nobody will know what happened up here," she said.

"That's why we need to return to Texsat immediately. To set the record straight. Can you get strapped in?" he said while turning to the door, reeling in the expandable airlock, and resealing it to the exit.

"I don't want to be alone," Christine said, moving across the cabin to assist him.

Soon they had the ship's compartments all closed up.

"You're not alone. I'm with you," said Jim.

"I mean down here," she said, looking at his frostbitten hand. She rubbed it, and he recoiled in pain.

"This doesn't look good," she said.

"All the more reason we need to get the hell off this cold, dead rock. Come sit with me in the cockpit."

Christine climbed up and settled into the small side seat as Jim tried to contact Texsat headquarters.

He turned on the communications system and only static came hissing through. "Radiation is disrupting the signal."

"Are we going to fly through it?" asked Christine.

"I only have fuel for one liftoff and a straight shot back to Earth. We have to go through it," he said while grabbing her hand in his. "You can stay here with me all the way home," he said.

"We're both going to die, aren't we?" she said.

"Not if I can prevent it," said Jim.

"Sooner than later. We took on too much radiation."

"I know a doctor in Dallas. He's a leader in immuno-therapy. I am not giving up hope that we can avoid the worst. I need to land us back home," he said.

"From your lips to God's ears," said Christine as the ground began to shake like a violent moonquake was starting.

"The mine!" screamed Christine.

"We leave now or we'll be buried alive!" he shouted while firing up the engines with his healthy hand. "Hang on tight." Jim skipped the system check and pressed the button for full ignition. The ship lurched upward, starting a slow climb made more difficult by being in the middle of a moondust storm.

They lifted off as a deep and long-lasting eruption from the center of the mine exploded, followed by con-tinuous nuclear blasts that obliterated the crater, causing it to collapse.

Jim had the TSLM at full speed and looked out at the expanding plume of pulverized moon rock and dust billow-ing from the base and pounding the ship with flying debris. Some chunks hit hard.

What was supposed to be a smooth low-gravity liftoff was a bumpy, uncertain race against thick gray clouds of pulverized dust.

Christine closed her eyes and kept praying, while Jim worked the spaceship as if it were a stick shift truck being coaxed over a steep hill. The pings and bangs from raining debris didn't stop them, and soon they were flying high above the Von Kármán crater and away from the new human-made crater deep inside it.

Jim tilted the TSLM and they both looked out the side viewport as they raced away from danger. All that remained was a deep black hole and a vortex of moon debris still exploding away from the hole. A new crater within a crater existed, and there would be no way to conceal it from people on Earth.

Moments later the TSLM broke away from the moon's small gravitational pull, rounding up the front side and heading straight for the blue planet. The only noise now was the gentle hum from the spaceship engine and interior systems. Christine's head listed gently as she fell asleep in the copilot's seat. Jim was also fading fast. He wouldn't have to assume manual control for another twenty-four hours. With the trajectory locked in, Jim reached over and held Christine's hand in his own. Moments later, he was also out like a light.

The TSLM and its two sleeping astronauts flew away from a moon forever altered by the first human battle on its surface and below.

A repetitive high-pitched beeping sound worked its way into Jim's dream. He was back in high school working at McDonald's. The fries were done, but he was unable to take the basket out of the oil because he was busy chatting up a beautiful girl at the drive-through window. The girl was Christine, and she was dressed in her spacesuit and her face was frostbitten.

"Do you want any sauces with your order?" said Jim.

"Jim, you need to wake up now," said Christine.

"How many?" he said.

"Wake up, Jim. What is this alarm? Please wake up," urged Christine as she lay on the horn of her car, which was really another loud alarm inside the ship.

Jim's eyes opened to see the instrument panel lit up before him. He rubbed his eyes and saw Earth through the viewport, extremely close and bright. He had slept too long. "Whoa!" Jim went into automatic mode and began pushing buttons to slow down the TSLM's approach. One by one the alarms went silent as the engine power was cut, and the TSLM fell into Earth's gravitational pull.

"We were coming in too fast. If you didn't wake me, we'd be melting soon," said Jim as he activated the heat shield and used the flight stick to begin a controlled descent toward the North Pole.

"Texsat Capcom, this is Spaceship Jim. Do you read me?" he said. A prolonged static silence was all that came back. "Texsat Capcom, this is Spaceship Jim. Do you—"

"Howdy Spaceship Jim. This is Texsat Capcom. It sure is good to hear your voice," crackled the voice of Dale York in the headset.

"I've got bad news. Only Christine and I made it back," said Jim.

"Only two survivors… I'm sorry Jim," said Capcom.

"The others gave their lives protecting America and the world. What's the situation on the ground?" said Jim.

"The whole world thinks a doomsday meteor slammed into the moon according to the news," said Capcom.

"That was no meteor," said Jim.

"We assumed as much and have been praying for your safety. The Air Force is standing by, waiting for me to relay your return flight path to them so they can assist you," said Capcom.

"Hold for flight path," said Jim while looking at his instrumentation.

"Roger. Standing by," said Capcom.

Jim exhaled and faced Christine who was looking at him. She had tears in her eyes and was emotionally and physically spent. The ship bumped and bounced as it neared the atmosphere.

"We're almost home… we're going to make it," he said.

"I hope so," she said.

"Capcom, we are entering Earth's atmosphere over Western Mongolia and have no choice but to pass right through Chinese airspace. We don't have enough fuel to orbit again and come in over America. We're entering south of Upper Mongolia, coming straight down past the South China Sea, across Japan, then Hawaii, and into the mainland before descending into Texas. I'm sending you the encrypted coordinates now," said Jim.

They waited in silence while the transmission was sent.

"Coordinates received. I'll notify the Pacific Command."

"Roger," said Jim. He flipped off the system and sat back and stared at Earth.

"What can I do now?" said Christine.

"Pray, hope, and don't worry," said Jim. He turned and smiled at her.

"Nothing will ever be the same down there now," she said.

"The world was already off its rails. I don't know what comes next, but I know I don't want to be a part of it," said Jim.

"What did we really get ourselves into?" she asked.

"I don't know anymore. Imagine if you never caught the boot print."

"The government knew more than was revealed. The Department of Energy machine had to be physically given to the Chinese somehow."

"Richard knew," said Jim. "He was a company man through and through, and with him gone, I'll never find out the truth."

"What will you do when we get home?"

"What do you mean?" he said.

"Nobody knows that I have the only processed helium-3 in existence, in my pocket. It's probably going to be the catalyst for the next world war, and I have it on me."

"What are you suggesting?" said Jim.

"That I find a way to throw it out before we arrive on Earth."

"But you said it's a clean future power source for the world."

"What are the chances you could develop a fusion rocket?"

Jim smiled at her. She was both crazy and incredibly attractive all at the same time.

"I have a few concepts. Why?"

"Because I'm only returning two H3 samples. I'm giving the third one to you."

"I wouldn't know how to make use of it."

"I do, and the situation on Earth might be beyond repair."

"The war is already happening. We were the perfect pawns in someone's geopolitical chess game," said Jim.

"Doesn't it make you mad?" Christine asked.

"You have no idea how it burns me."

"What if you could build a ship so we could leave this godforsaken planet and go live peacefully on another world?"

"The closest star system to our own, with habitable planets like ours, is ten light-years away and there's no guarantee it's more peaceful than Earth."

"I know, but one can dream, right?" she said.

"You also know we would be dead long before even getting out of our own solar system," he said.

"I understand that too."

"Why even suggest something as far-fetched as interplanetary travel?" he said.

"Because I have seen what you're capable of. Maybe you're the first person who can invent a working warp drive, maybe we need to make alien contact so humans will stop fighting one another," she said.

"You're delirious, Christine. Talk to me again when we're back on the ground and you've had a restful sleep," he said while pressing a few buttons and adjusting the flight stick. Suddenly, the ship started shaking violently.

"What's wrong now?" said Christine.

Jim struggled with the flight stick. He was using both hands to try and keep it steady as the ship started to roll. "Some of the internal stabilizers broke down, and in zero gravity we didn't feel a thing. Now we're entering the atmo-sphere and we're feeling it," he said taking deep breaths to remain calm.

The ship slammed against the atmosphere, and fire started cascading across the viewports.

Jim looked at Christine and pointed to a panel to her right. "You see the green switch right there?" Jim was pull-ing hard on both flight sticks, trying to manually control the ship.

"This one right here?" said Christine with her finger hovering over it.

"Flip it down!" he said.

She pressed it down and the ship shuddered as Jim flipped and pressed other buttons on his left-hand side while still holding the flight stick with his right. The shak-ing intensified. Jim looked at Christine. A reflection of the red flames cascaded over her face. She smiled meekly at him.

"Brace for the sound barrier," said Jim.

Kaboom! They broke through the atmosphere, the ship looked like a streaking comet across the daytime sky high above Mongolia.

Wen Jun must have gotten word back to Beijing before his ship was destroyed because within seconds of entering the upper atmosphere, five People's Liberation Air Force fighter jets were rocketing straight up toward his position.

"We've got company," Jim said.

Christine saw the approaching jets, noticing the streak-ing missiles heading their way.

"They're trying to blow us right out of the sky," she said.

"Well they can kiss my freedom-loving American butt!" said Jim as he let out a wild yell and sent the ship diving toward the ground instead of following a smooth arc over the globe. Missiles fired right past them as Jim corkscrewed out of the way, smashing into one another and creating a cluster explosion above the TSLM.

Fighter jets blew by, yards above them, breaking off in four different directions—two looped up and around, one looped left, another looped right, and the last fighter looped down, closing in on the TSLM like a horizontal flying crane claw. A cat-and-dog fight between the PLAAF's best pilots and Jim from Texas in his battered spaceship carried on for an intense four minutes of bobbing, weaving, and evading trained pilots' direct attacks.

Christine held on and screamed with each terrifying roll. While upside down she witnessed two fighter jets collide, both spinning in flames down to the ground. The TSLM rocketed across Chinese airspace, soon to cross into the safety of the Sea of Japan.

"C'mon... where're our boys at," said Jim.

That's when four American stealth bombers rose up from nowhere and flew in tight formation under and above Jim's ship. One bomber took up the rear so the TSLM was defended on three sides.

"Welcome home, Jim. You are now safe in American-controlled airspace and under the escort and protection of the Pacific Command. Those Chicoms won't bother you no more. We're gonna stay by your side all the way to Texas," said one of the pilots.

"Copy. It's good to be home. I thank God for you guys and that we made it," said Jim.

"From what I hear, we need to thank you. You took the teeth right out of the dragon's mouth," said the pilot.

"Don't mention it," said Jim.

They flew in a solid formation across the Pacific, passing over the Hawaiian Islands, crossing California, and on toward Texas, where the stealth bombers broke away and disappeared.

"Capcom this is Spaceship Jim about to make my initial descent. Prepare the landing zone for arrival," said Jim.

"LZ is ready and rescue crews are standing by," said Capcom.

Fire trucks, military hazmat, and rescue vehicles were gathered around the landing zone but at a safe distance. Dozens of Texsat and military personnel were awaiting the arrival of the TSLM. Choppers hovered in the air.

A roaring sound echoed across the valley, and the TSLM dropped down into the horizon like a fiery chariot from heaven, slow moving, engines burning off the last of the fuel, rapid firing as it reoriented to a vertical position. Dust billowed as it descended slowly, creating a thick fog around the LZ. The rocket engines fired and popped. Strange sounds came through the dust.

"Touchdown!" said Jim. Heavy smoke and dust swirled around the viewport windows making it seem as dark as evening outside. Jim leaned his head forward and started to sob.

Christine moved closer and hugged him. "Thank you," she said.

"Jimmy?" said Capcom.

"Yes, sir," said Jim.

"I hope you understand. You and Dr. Uy are being transported to a military hospital for medical evaluation.

They want to take the TSLM too because of the radioactivity," said Capcom.

"I understand… it's the right thing to do."

"We may never retrieve the TSLM again," said Capcom.

"Bill them for it," said Jim.

"Already did. I'll see you in a minute," said Capcom.

The dust settled. A windowless white van drove toward the TSLM and stopped short. Two MPs in hazmat suits got out from the back and approached the spaceship door. It flung open, and Jim and Christine stood there, squinting their eyes in the blinding sun. Both a mess and sickly looking. The sudden gravity and searing heat made Jim pass out and tumble forward, landing face down on the Texas ground.

"No!" said Christine as she jumped down to help, but was stopped by an MP while the other MP pulled Jim's body off the ground and into the van. Christine was ordered to climb in after him. The MP pulled the doors closed, and the van turned around and drove out of the Texsat compound.

Fire trucks pulled up and began hosing down the TSLM with a white foam to bring the temperature down. After the bath, a small army of hazmat-suit-wearing MPs started wrapping the TSLM in a white parachute-like fabric, while a huge crane and a flatbed truck pulled up. The military was moving at a breakneck pace to move the TSLM off the compound and hidden from sight.

Jance and Colonel Stetz were also in the back of the van wearing hazmat suits. They sat on opposite sides of the gurneys that Jim and Christine were being treated on by two military medics who were busy removing their boots.

"How do you feel, Dr. Uy?" Jance said to Christine.

"I've seen better days," said Christine.

"Who are you? Have we met?" said Jim to Colonel Stetz.

"My name's Lou. I'm the CIA point man Richard worked with on your project. I need to know what happened up there, every detail you two can remember while the events are still fresh in your mind."

"Starting when?" said Jim.

"Starting with the moment you touched down," said Stetz.

While Stetz listened to Jim recall the mission, Christine had managed to work the H3 disks out of her pocket without being seen. She reached for Jance and palmed them into his hand.

"What's this?" said Jance.

"Hide it," whispered Christine.

Jance nodded, glanced down rather puzzled at the H3 disks in black cases, then slid them next to his calf, between his hazmat suit tucked into his boots.

The medic working on Christine cut her spacesuit arm open and disinfected her wrist. "A little pinch," he said as he inserted an IV into her arm.

"What's that for?"

"You're severely dehydrated."

Christine rolled her head to the side to look at Jim talking to Stetz.

"And that's when we had our first real setback. Kyle's fall trying to scale down into the Von Kármán. It left him badly wounded until we could administer medical help and the best place for that was inside the base," said Jim.

"How big was the entire moon base, your best estimate?" said Stetz.

"At least two thousand acres."

"What an absolute miracle that you survived," said Stetz.

"We should both be dead," said Jim.

Stetz looked over at Christine as she was getting her needle adjusted.

"How about you, Dr. Uy? What did you find up there?" said Stetz.

Jim reached for her hand and squeezed it. They looked into one another's eyes while the medical team cut away their bloody spacesuits.

"I found the future," said Christine, looking into Jim's eyes. He knew exactly what she meant and smiled at her.

The white van drove up the long gravel road and out of the valley, escorted by two black helicopters, leaving the Texsat compound behind in a cloud of dust.

THE END.